Trophy Kill

Trophy Kill

A SIDNEY REED NOVEL

R.J. NORGARD

Bird Dog Publishing
Huron, Ohio

Bird Dog Publishing
An imprint of Bottom Dog Press, Inc.
P.O. Box 425
Huron, Ohio/44839
http://smithdocs.net/bird_dog_books

ISBN 978-1-9475-0415-8
Printed in the United States of America

for Suzy

Three may keep a secret if two of them are dead.

—Ben Franklin

Prologue

Dawn breaks to the bubble and murmur of the mighty Nushagak River. Somewhere in the distance, a loon's haunting cry pierces the chill morning air. As if in reply, a bull moose lumbers to his feet, stretches his long powerful legs, and shakes off a fine layer of frost.

Standing eight feet at the shoulder and weighing three-quarters of a ton, he appears awkward and ungainly, but he can outrun a mature grizzly if need be. The antlers resting atop his head weigh fifty pounds and span six feet from tip to tip. He has survived many battles, as the scars crisscrossing his dusky hide attest.

With a shake of his massive head, he stalks off through the low-bush willow.

Three miles away, near the bank of a narrow creek, woodsmoke drifts lazily skyward from a crackling campfire. Bacon sizzles in a large iron skillet as steam rises from a copper kettle. A beefy, broad-shouldered man in a heavy wool coat cracks an egg and spills its contents into the skillet as his two companions look on hungrily, sipping coffee from tin cups.

"Today's the day, boys," the big man says, turning the bacon with a fork.

"You said that yesterday," one of the men say.

"I came to get a moose and that's what I'm gonna do," the big man replies with conviction.

The third man sips coffee and says, "What's our strategy?"

"We're gonna hit that big ridge to the north," the big man says. "He's in there for sure. We've seen his sign."

"Yeah, we've heard that before, too," the third man grins.

"Okay," the big man says, "let's get shaking."

Amid grunts of agreement, the men dowse the fire and prepare for the day's hunt. Ten minutes later, rifles slung over their shoulders, they trudge off single file.

The moose drinks leisurely at the river's edge, pausing frequently to sniff the air, before turning inland in search of willing females. He senses his dominance in this valley, though he knows an upstart rival could challenge him at any moment. He is also watchful for predators. His only natural enemies are the wolf and the grizzly. He is confident he can hold his own against these threats. There is also the distant memory of an encounter with a strange two-legged animal, but that was a long time ago.

Pausing at the edge of a clearing, he scrapes bare a two-foot-square patch of earth and urinates into it. Like an olfactory calling card, the urine's musky odor drifts away on tendrils of air, announcing his presence to any females roaming nearby. He snorts and bellows in a raw display of male bravado.

By mid-morning the three hunters have walked almost five miles, following a pre-planned route that will lead them to a ridge affording them an unobstructed view of the valley below. The route they are on is a circuitous one, designed by the big man guiding them to keep them downwind of their quarry.

The big man stops and holds up a beefy palm. The faint murmur of rippling water rises from the bramble. He turns to face the men following him. "This is the spot. He'll work his way up this drainage. We'll take up a stand along a line parallel to the creek and intercept him when he comes through." He points to a section of open ground, slightly elevated, to their left. "I'll head up that ridge beyond the clearing. Try to keep fifty or sixty yards between you, but don't lose sight of each other."

Another man glances around, looking anxious. "The wind is all over the place. If he smells us, this day will be another big zero."

The others nod. Silently they disperse along the creek.

The bull stops dead in his tracks. A fresh scent teases his sensitive nostrils, triggering fearful memories of long ago. The source of the hated scent is the strange two-legged animal that strikes from afar, wounding with a fierce and burning fire.

His muscles tense. Blind rage rises and engulfs every fiber of his being. The urge to rut is overridden by an even more primal instinct: survival. To kill or be killed. And so he waits.

His wait is not long. His keen olfactory powers discern three two-legged predators. He listens for the rustling of leaves, the snap of a branch. His ears pan left and right, triangulating sounds, calculating range and direction.

He inches forward, alert to the faintest movement. Pausing at the edge of a clearing, he leans his majestic head out cautiously. There, at the far end of the clearing, the object of his wrath falls into focus. His dull black eyes grow wide.

Lowering his head, the rage-filled beast lunges into the open ground, long sinewy legs pumping like pistons, each thunderous footfall closing the distance. In seconds he is midway through the clearing. An ear-splitting *crack!* stabs his eardrums, followed instantly by a searing heat in his left shoulder. Still he charges, fueled by adrenalin and rage, his only thought unleashing death upon the dark figure looming before him.

Two years later

One

Swatting the snooze button for the third time, it dawned on me that the pounding I'd been hearing was coming from my front door and not my head. I rolled over and squinted at the alarm clock on my nightstand: 9:20 a.m.

Why do people feel the need to get up so early?

I lay still, listening, temples throbbing from one too many Coronas. The gentle strumming of a guitar drifted up from the coffee shop one floor below.

More pounding.

"Go away," I moaned to no one.

Still more pounding.

Crap. This isn't going to stop.

Easing my forty-five-year-old body into a sitting position, I threw on the holey jeans and sweatshirt I'd left crumpled on the floor the night before and dragged my feet from the bedroom to the front door. Peering through the peephole, I spied a strikingly attractive woman with shoulder-length blond hair who looked to be in her mid-to-late thirties. No sign of a portfolio or clipboard.

Not a saleswoman. Still...

I unlatched the door and eased it open. Definitely a total babe. She looked me up and down, displaying less disapproval than I would have expected from a woman of apparent substance.

"Are you Sidney Reed, the detective?"

"We don't use that word around here."

"We?"

"I have a cat."

Her eyes narrowed. Without waiting for an invitation, she

breezed past me and I caught a hint of sweet perfume. The good stuff. I was at once miffed at and intrigued by her boldness.

This could be interesting.

She scanned the room, seeming to take it all in with a casual glance. Then again, there wasn't much to take in: overstuffed couch, end table, chair, coffee table for propping up my feet, small-screen TV, large bookcase stuffed with volumes of every shape and description, and, in a lonely corner of the room, an antique rocking chair being taken up by Priscilla, my somewhat overweight black cat.

I cursed myself for leaving a pizza box and empty beer bottles on the coffee table. I wasn't accustomed to visitors, especially those of the female knockout persuasion.

I shut the door behind her. "How can I help you, Miss . . ."

"Landers. Elizabeth Landers. I'll come straight to the point, Mr. Reed. I want you to follow my fiancé."

It took a moment for that to register in my beer-addled brain. "You've been misinformed, Miss Landers. I'm retired. Anyway, how did you find me? I'm not listed."

"My attorney, Eddie Baker, told me you're the best private detec—uh, investigator in Alaska." She glanced around the room, her gaze lingering on the Corona bottles. "Although, frankly, I'm having a hard time believing him."

There was a time in the not-too-distant past when her comment would have pissed me off. Those were the days.

I squinted at her through puffy eyelids. "Eddie Baker sent you?"

"Yes."

Eddie Baker is the most colorful, if not gifted, attorney in Alaska. I'd done a lot of work for Eddie and considered him a friend, though I hadn't seen him in months. It bothered me that he had told this woman where I lived without asking me.

"In that case, I'm sorry you wasted your time. I'll be happy to refer you—"

"No one else will do. I'm prepared to offer you a generous retainer if you help me."

Not only was she beautiful, she was also persistent.

"I'm sorry. I'm sure you'll be—"

"I'll pay you in cash."

Beautiful, persistent, *and* smart. My checking account was hemorrhaging money faster than oil from the *Exxon Valdez* oil tanker. This might be a chance to earn some easy cash and pay my landlady.

"Where are my manners? Please sit down. I'm not saying I'll take the case, but there's no harm in listening to what you have to say. Can I get you a cup of coffee?"

"Black. No sugar. Please, call me Elizabeth."

"Call me Sidney." I gestured toward the rocker and the blob of black fur lying in repose. "By the way, that's Priscilla. I'll be right back."

She nodded. "All right, Sidney."

I gestured toward my faded yet remarkably cozy sofa and headed for the kitchen. I drained the black sludge that remained in the pot from earlier in the week. After firing up the coffee maker, I took my first good look at Elizabeth Landers through the kitchen doorway.

She had an angular face with high cheekbones. She wore an off-white pants suit and matching vest that showcased her fit body. Her ocean blue eyes were sparkling yet guarded. I imagined that in high school she could have been both class president and head cheerleader, easily able to make the transition from one to the other. As I watched her, a cherry red handbag on her lap and a let's-get-down-to-business look on her face, I decided I liked her.

When the coffee maker stopped sputtering, I poured the steamy dark liquid into a pair of mugs, each bearing the colorful image of a goofy-looking moose. I'd bought a set of four at a thrift shop right after I moved in here nine months ago.

Returning to the living room, I handed her one of the mugs and sat down opposite her. She looked it over as if inspecting for cooties, took a tentative first sip, and said, "I've never hired a detective before. How does this work?"

"My fee is seventy-five dollars an hour, with a non-refundable, one-thousand-dollar retainer up front—if I decide to take the case."

Her response was immediate and nonchalant. She reached into her handbag, pulled out a roll of bills, and dealt ten crisp one-hundred-dollar notes into my palm.

I stared at them, trying not to be impressed. "Thank you, but—"

"Please. I'm confident you'll take the case."

"Fine. I'll write you a receipt."

"That won't be necessary. I'd just as soon get started."

I tucked the money in my jeans and looked around for something to write on. I spied a dog-eared writing pad and pencil under the coffee table.

"All right, Elizabeth. Tell me about your fiancé."

She folded her hands neatly on her lap. "Harvey and I have been dating for about six months, although I've known him since high school. He moved in with me three months ago."

"Harvey?"

"I'm sorry. Kahill. Harvey Kahill."

I scribbled the name on the pad, hoping she didn't notice the slight shake in my hand.

"Please continue," I said.

Her brow furrowed. "He's been behaving strangely the past several weeks. Irritable. Keeping to himself. He seems . . . troubled. When I ask him what's wrong, he won't say. He retreats to his workshop. At first, I thought he was still grieving over Tom."

"Tom?"

Her gaze dropped to her lap. "Tom Landers, my late husband. He was killed two years ago on a moose-hunting trip with Harvey and a friend of theirs, Joe Meacham. You may have read about it. The story made the front page of the Daily News."

I thought back a few years. Death in the wild is common in Alaska. Hardly a week goes by without someone tumbling down a mountainside, crashing a plane, or falling prey to a grizzly. Tom Landers' name didn't ring any immediate bells.

"I'm sorry for your loss. What happened?"

She set her mug on the table. "They were stalking a bull moose in dense brush. The moose charged at Tom. Joe managed to get off a shot and bring him down, but it was . . . too late."

She looked away and I thought I saw the beginnings of a tear. I glanced at her coffee mug moose, wanting to slap the silly grin off its face. I suddenly felt the need for aspirin. To fill the awkward silence, I said, "So you want me to follow Harvey to find out what's troubling him?"

She stared at her cup. "Harvey and I have a daily routine. We eat dinner around six o'clock, afterwards retiring to the family room for a drink. Two weeks ago Friday, something changed."

I leaned forward. "What changed?"

"After dinner, without explanation, Harvey drove off in his truck. He came back two hours later without so much as a word about where'd he'd been. He wouldn't even look at me."

"Has he ever done anything like that before?"

"No. It's not like him at all. The following week—Friday last—it was exactly the same, except . . ."

"Except what?"

"This time he took a gun with him."

"How do you know?"

"I hugged him as he was leaving. I felt it."

"You're sure?"

She shot me a withering look. "Sidney, please don't insult my intelligence. I grew up around guns. I know what one feels like. I implored him not to go, but it was no use. He returned a few hours later, refusing to discuss it. When I pressed him, he mumbled something about needing some air. Then he hurried to his shop. I brought it up again later, but he absolutely refused to discuss it. It's so odd because Harvey has always been very open with me. Always."

"Could he be seeing someone else?"

She shook her head before I'd finished the question. "If there's one thing I'm sure of, it's Harvey's fidelity. No, it must be something else."

"Has he received any unusual phone calls or mail?"

She shook her head.

"Any other change in his routine?"

"Not that I know of, but then he spends most of the day at the office."

In response to my questioning look, she said, "He owns a business here in Anchorage, Aurora Electronics Supply."

I nodded, recalling that I'd been in the place a few times. I wrote down the name.

"Has there been any unusual behavior so far this week?"

"He's been quiet and moody but hasn't gone anywhere. Not like that."

I mused, "Interesting that he left the house on consecutive Fridays. You're thinking he'll leave again tomorrow?"

"I'm afraid I think he will."

I paused, recalling with sadness the last time I'd done surveillance. It was a night I'd never forget as long as I lived.

"All right," I said with a sigh. I glanced at the scenic Alaska calendar tacked to the wall next to the television, noting that, like the other twenty-nine days in the month, I had no appointments. "I'll watch the house tomorrow. If he goes anywhere, I'll tag along."

She nodded in gratitude.

I sipped from my mug and said, "I need you to provide me some more information about Harvey: physical description, vehicles, the route he takes to the store, drinking buddies, high school sweethearts. Full names, addresses, phone numbers. When in doubt, assume I need it."

"It may take me a while. How soon do you need it?"

World War III was raging in my head and I needed time to negotiate a cease-fire. I said, "By the end of the day would be fine."

"I'll have it for you this afternoon."

"Good." I sipped some more coffee. "Ordinarily, I would have a contract for you to sign, but I'm afraid I'm . . . fresh out of forms."

"Not to worry. A handshake suits me just fine."

"Me, too." We shook hands and I walked her to the door.

"Will you be in this afternoon?" she wanted to know.

"If I'm not, you can slide your notes under the door."

She placed a hand on my shoulder. "I can't thank you enough, Sidney." Her face clouded. "I fear he's gotten himself mixed up in something." Then she walked out the door.

After she'd gone, I headed for the kitchen and picked up an aspirin bottle lying on the counter, twisted off the cap, and tapped four white tablets into the palm of my hand. Filling a green plastic tumbler with tap water, I returned to the sofa and plopped myself down. Priscilla joined me, settling snugly in the center of my lap. I placed the aspirin on my tongue and raised the tumbler in a mock toast. "Here's to this month's rent."

I swallowed hard as the tepid water slid down my throat.

Two

For the better part of a year, I'd been content to languish inside, only venturing out from time to time to stock up on supplies or bend an elbow down at the Prospector Bar. The sole exception to this routine was my daily trip downstairs to the Mighty Moose Café for a tall mocha—one of the few remnants of my former life still intact. Perhaps it was my way of retaining a modicum of sanity.

The Mighty Moose is a fixture in downtown Anchorage, a magnet for a small but loyal clientele of lawyers, paralegals, shop owners, and office workers. Its eclectic menu of exotic coffees and teas, poppy seed muffins, and fresh-made quiche is etched in colored chalk above the counter. The small interior features half a dozen round, ornately decorated wooden tables encircled by scuffed wooden chairs. I like to tease the owner that she must have found the furnishings on a scavenger hunt gone awry. For some reason, she doesn't think that's as funny as I do.

I donned brown striped socks and penny loafers and traipsed down the rickety stairs that clung to my apartment building like a drowning man to a life ring. It was the first day of September. A morning chill, propelled by a stiff breeze off Cook Inlet, slapped me in the face like an angry lover as I descended to street level, though the sun's rays felt damn good caressing my face. In another two months, I knew, the sun would languish anemically above the horizon, too low in the sky to provide more than a token expression of heat.

I paused to drink in the bracing Alaskan air, remembering the first time I'd done that. How new and exciting it all seemed then. The Last Frontier. Land of indescribable beauty and boundless opportunity. Had someone asked me then if there were anywhere else I'd rather be, I would have replied with an emphatic "no." But now it seemed cold and unforgiving and a thousand miles from nowhere. For the moment though, the greenbacks in my pocket felt good, the aspirin had done their work well, and I sauntered into the coffee shop with a rare air of confidence. I stepped up to the counter just as a young brunette in a snappy business suit scooped up her latte and headed for a table. I pegged her for an attorney, no doubt one of the newbies at the public defender's office, fresh out of Northeastern.

She'll learn soon enough.

I took a deep breath, savoring the aroma of fresh coffee. Behind the counter stood a slightly stocky woman with flaming red hair, decked out in faded blue jeans and a green plaid shirt—traditional Alaskan attire. Rachel Saint George looked like a sixties flower child, her curly locks festooned with brightly colored ribbons. She was the owner of the café, my landlady, and for reasons I could not fathom had made looking after me her pet project.

Rachel eyed me suspiciously. "Well, Sidney," she began in her trademark husky voice. "You're grinning like it's your birthday. Or did you just win the lottery?"

"In a manner of speaking. I picked up a job this morning."

Her sapphire eyes widened. "Will wonders never cease? Well, whatever funds you received you can hand over to me." Her eyes trailed down my left arm to the hand clutching the wad of bills Elizabeth had given me, minus one of the C notes. "Is that what I think it is?"

"Why yes, Rachel, it's a subscription to that men's magazine you've been wanting."

"Ass. You know damn well I'm talking about rent. That's two months you're behind now. Here I am, letting you have the upstairs apartment at a bargain basement price, and this is the thanks I get."

"It's only fair. I feel like I'm living in a basement."

She grabbed at the money and I jerked it away from her a time or two just as she reached for it—I wanted to make the moment last—before letting her have it. With a look of feigned indignation she counted out the bills.

I said, "That's two months' rent."

"It's about time," she said, placing the money in a drawer.

I wasn't done with her quite yet. "So, tell me, Rachel, how is it that you and I never married?"

She launched a mortified look in my direction. "I don't know. Why don't you ask my girlfriend the next time you see her?"

I feigned shock. "Girlfriend? How am I supposed to compete with that?"

"You can't," she grinned.

Just as she teased me about my reclusive lifestyle, so I teased her endlessly about her preference in companions, though not nearly as much as she and her life partner, Beatrice, teased each other.

"So, are you going to order something or did you just come down to gloat?"

"Gloat, mostly. But since I'm here anyway, I may as well order something."

"The usual?"

I scratched my chin. "No, I think I'm in the mood to splurge. Give me the venti."

"Praise Jesus, now I can retire."

I stood there grinning. As out of whack as my life seemed, Rachel could always make me smile. I needed that in my life at the moment. Truth be told, I don't know if I would have survived these last months without her.

A few minutes later she placed a chocolate-brown coffee mug on the counter. "Here you go, master detective."

I picked up the mug and a newspaper lying on the counter and wandered off to my favorite table near the window, where

I settled into the least rickety of three chairs. I glanced around and noticed the twenty-something gal had her head buried in her newspaper and there were now three new customers waiting their turn at the counter. Unfolding my paper, I ignored the world news and paged over to the local section. Alaska news is no different than anywhere else—absurd and violent and not all that interesting. I thumbed through the pages looking for familiar names, a habit I'd picked up when I was a thriving P.I. Though I was no longer thriving, old habits die hard. On this day I saw none.

Such has been my routine since Molly died. On that day my life went into a tailspin from which it had yet to recover. I sold the house—why have one if there's no one to share it with?—and went looking for an apartment. In my years doing P.I. work the Mighty Moose Café had become a welcome hangout and Rachel a good friend. I recalled her having an apartment above the cafe she'd been trying to rent out. A quick call told me it was still available. So here I was, living off a rapidly deflating savings account, Coronas, coffee, and sarcasm.

Until that day I had been at the top of my game, commanding the respect of the legal community and my fellow investigators. Mostly I did legal investigations, both criminal and civil, for half a dozen attorneys who made up my client list. The remainder of my work came from the phone book. Domestics, mostly. In a typical domestic case, the client suspects their partner of cheating. The P.I.'s job—my job—is to catch them at it. I was effective and reliable. Until Molly died, that is. That's when I stopped returning phone calls, and in this business, that's a reputation killer. My phone stopped ringing.

I lifted the mug to my lips and sipped gratefully. My thoughts drifted to Elizabeth Landers. When she handed me the money and I held those crisp hundred-dollar bills in my hands, it had felt good. Not just having the money but having the work—any work. I missed it more than I cared to admit.

I took another sip and stared out the window. The late morning sun, sunk low in the southern sky, peeked around the corners of the buildings. In contemptuous disregard for the calendar, Old Man Winter typically grips the state in his cold, bony fingers by late September or early October—there's no waiting for December here. Word was, though, that the Winter thing was coming even earlier this year than normal.

September is also moose hunting season. By now, hunters were preparing to head into the bush in hopes of bagging their annual moose and filling their freezers with meat for the long winter months.

I drained the bottom of my mug. Maybe it was finally time to move on. Perhaps a simple surveillance was all I needed to get my life back on track.

A simple surveillance. Now there's a contradiction in terms.

Three

I returned to my apartment hoping to straighten the place up a bit before Elizabeth returned with her notes. The look on her face when she'd seen the mess on my coffee table reminded me that Molly had been a diligent housekeeper, always picking up after me without complaint. I bagged the beer bottles, pizza box, and dirty napkins, and even ran my thrift store vacuum cleaner. Observing from her rocking chair perch, Priscilla eyed me as though I were a creature from another planet.

That bit of menial labor triggered my appetite so I donned a gray hoodie and tromped back downstairs to G Street. It was bright and sunny—unusual for September. Rain is the norm this time of year. I glanced up at the Chugach Mountains to the east to see how far the snow—Alaskans call it "termination dust"—had descended down the mountainside. I guessed the snow line to be at about the four-thousand-foot level. In a few more weeks, the white stuff would be dusting Anchorage streets.

Newcomers to Alaska—we call them *cheechakos* up here—are truly perplexed by the seasons. The calendar notwithstanding, Alaska has about a month each of spring and fall, barely three months of summer, and the rest is winter—cold, dark, and never-ending. Did I mention cold?

I strolled north the short distance to Third Avenue and hung a right toward the Hilton, where a gaggle of tourists—notable for their extra-heavy coats and lost expressions—were milling around outside. By this time of year most of the tourists have retreated down the ALCAN—the Alaska-Canada Highway—in their tour buses and Winnebagos, back to their nine-to-fives, boring their friends silly with tales of adventure, complete with photos of mountains and glaciers. But there were still a few around, taking advantage of cheap off-season room rates.

At the Hilton, I hung another right, walked south on E Street, then turned right on Fourth. You wouldn't know it these days, but the downtown area was devastated in 1964 when nature ushered in its own brand of urban renewal in the form of a 9.2 earthquake. Since the 1950s, Fourth Avenue had been infamous as Anchorage's "Tenderloin District"—a mecca for gambling and prostitution—lined with bars with names like The Wild Cherry and Captain Ahab's. Racketeers, pimps, drug dealers, and low-lifes flourished. Today the avenue was tame by comparison, the bars and gambling dens and whorehouses converted into gift shops, restaurants, and government buildings. The bars remain, though they're a bit tamer these days.

A familiar aroma teased my nostrils. I crossed over to the south side of the street, where a hot dog vendor stood behind a stainless-steel cart, piling onions sautéed in Coca Cola onto a bratwurst with a pair of silver tongs. The dog vendors are an institution in Anchorage during the summer months. The municipality rents out various locations—at a premium, of course—with a dozen vendors vying for the choicest spots. I stepped into line and after a short wait ordered a reindeer dog smothered in onions, a bag of chips, and a soda. While Jeff worked his magic on the grill, we chatted about the coming moose-hunting season and rumors of an early winter.

In due course, he slid the dog into a hoagie roll and wrapped it in tinfoil. I gathered up my lunch, walked back across the street, and sat down on a gray concrete bench outside the old federal courthouse building. As I wolfed down the first bite of my dog, I looked up to see attorney Eddie Baker striding toward me, his gray pinstripe suit flapping open. The flamboyant lawyer was tall, tanned, and lean. I made no effort to stand.

"Sidney! Where have you been hiding?" he said, extending his right hand.

I set my hot dog down next to me and returned his greeting. "Taking some time off, Eddie. Heard about your win in the Steinberger case. Congratulations."

"Thanks, Sid. Missed you on that one."

"I heard Dena did one helluva job for you." Dena Williams, an Anchorage P.I., had been my main competition in the criminal defense community. She was a decent investigator, but she lacked imagination. A good investigator has to be creative.

"She got it done, all right, but you're still my favorite." He paused, studying me. "Look," he said at last, "I know you've been going through a difficult time, but at some point you've got to get back to work. What's it been? Nine, ten months?"

"Something like that."

"That's long enough. You need to work. In fact, just yesterday I gave you a referral."

"Yeah, thanks for the heads-up, Eddie," I said with only slightly disguised sarcasm.

"Hey, figured you could use the work." He sat down next to me on the cold cement. I felt his eyes on me as I bit into my dog. I sensed what was coming.

"I was sorry to hear about Molly. That was a bad deal all around. She was a nice lady."

The concrete bench seemed much colder all of a sudden. I was staring at my feet when I heard Eddie speak.

"Now listen, be sure and take good care of Elizabeth. She's a nice lady and she always pays." He leaned closer and elbowed me in the arm. "And she's pretty nice to look at, too."

"I'll take good care of her, Eddie." I raised three fingers. "Scout's honor."

He glanced at his Rolex and jumped to his feet. "Hell's bells, buddy. I've gotta get to court. Remember what I said, Sid. I've got plenty of work. When you're ready, give me a call."

Eddie turned and dashed off down Fourth Avenue in the direction of the courthouse. I picked up my reindeer dog and watched him go. With his jacket flapping at his sides, he reminded me of a gangly gray bird.

When I returned to my apartment at a quarter past one, I was surprised to find a manila envelope on the floor just inside the door. A note written across the front said: *Sidney, I trust this is all the information you require. Elizabeth*

I tore open the envelope to find a yellow legal pad, its pages covered in elegant handwriting, and a photograph of a man sitting on a park bench. Harvey was more distinguished looking than handsome, with dark, thinning hair and a roundish face. A pair of dark, horn-rimmed glasses made him look bookish. I saw casual confidence, though not arrogance. Setting the photo aside, I read the carefully handwritten pages. It was all there—a detailed physical description of Harvey, people he knew, places he might go, habits, favorite sports, vehicle information, everything. Her notes filled a dozen pages.

Damn, she whipped this out fast.

After shrugging off my coat, I grabbed a beer from the fridge and settled into the sofa with Priscilla and the legal pad. It was time to do my homework on Harvey Kahill.

After graduating from McKinley High School in Anchorage, Harvey cranked out a business degree from the University of Alaska Anchorage before starting Aurora Electronics Supply. About that same time he married his high school sweetheart, Gloria Gifford. She divorced him after eight years of an increasingly stale marriage with nothing to show for it except alimony payments. Outside the home, Harvey's life revolved around his two long-time friends, Joe Meacham and Tom Landers, and their outdoor adventures. Joe was a pilot who owned a guide service based at Lake Hood near Anchorage International Airport, which made him the go-to guy for the group's outdoor adventures. Harvey had other casual friends, but Tom and Joe formed his inner circle. I amused myself by mentally dubbing them the "Three Amigos." I could almost picture them in sombreros.

Elizabeth noted, in her elegant script, that Harvey had taken the passing of his friend Tom Landers hard. I paused to take a swig of beer, my thoughts drifting to Tom's death. I couldn't help but wonder how she felt about dating her late husband's best friend. That had to be awkward.

I put down the file. Priscilla seized the opportunity and pounced on my now-empty lap. I scratched her chin and drank some more beer. On a blank sheet of paper I made a list of information I would need to know on the fly—names and addresses of his friends and the establishments they frequented, vehicle license plate numbers, and so on. This would serve as my "cheat sheet" while on surveillance. I stuffed the papers back into the envelope and tossed it on the coffee table.

My last order of business was to scope out the area around the Landers' home. Few things are more embarrassing than waiting for hours on end for the "rabbit" to appear, only to discover later they'd taken a route you hadn't known existed.

I revved up my notebook computer—which, along with a small inkjet printer, was one of the few high-tech remnants of my past life—and pulled up a map of Elizabeth's address. (One of the unanticipated perks of living above Rachel's coffee shop was free Wi-Fi.) I printed out maps of the area around her home and stuffed them into the envelope—now my makeshift case file.

I said goodbye to Priscilla before heading to the parking garage, where I kept my worse-for-wear forest green Subaru Outback all-wheel drive. My clients, whose collective image of the modern detective is based on what they read in novels or see on television, are invariably disappointed that I don't drive a Ferrari. For that matter, so am I. But when I'm following someone through the city on ice-covered roads, I'm thankful to have the Subaru. To further burnish its credentials as a kick-ass surveillance vehicle, I'd had the windows tinted and made a point of not washing it too often. It's the kind of car you can leave parked in a neighborhood for hours without arousing suspicion.

Harvey and Elizabeth resided in an area of Anchorage known as the Hillside, which, as its name implies, lies in the foothills of the Chugach Mountains to the east of the city. Its residents, who occupy some of the most sought-after real estate within the municipality of Anchorage, look out over—and some would say down upon—the city below. They also enjoy a commanding view of Cook Inlet and its adjoining inlet, Turnagain Arm, to the north and west.

Maneuvering through light pre-rush-hour traffic, I guided the Subaru south on the Seward Highway, exited at Huffman Boulevard, and turned east toward the mountains. Beyond the relative flatness of the city proper, Huffman climbed steadily for several miles before rising sharply where it merged with the mountains. From there I zigzagged through countless switch-backs, past countless side streets, gradually gaining in elevation until, finally, I arrived at the home of Elizabeth Landers.

The place was impressive enough to stand out in a neigh-borhood where grand is the norm. A semi-circular driveway led to a beige split-level home, with rustic wood siding, forest-green trim, and an attached three-car garage. Perfectly trimmed hedges and a neat row of stately birch trees bordered a perfectly trimmed lawn. A wrought-iron fence surrounded the property, completing this picture of Alaskan-style opulence.

I continued past the residence for a quarter mile before arriving at a dead end, confirming what I'd surmised earlier from checking the maps: there was only one way out. So far, so good. All that remained was finding a spot from which to observe Harvey leaving his driveway without sticking out like a sore thumb. On my second pass, I found a small clearing among a grove of trees about a hundred feet from the gate that afforded both an unobstructed view of the house and sufficient cover for my car. I backed into the spot and sat there a moment. It offered adequate though not ideal concealment. It would do.

I drove back to the last turnoff, turned around, and drove

past the house one more time, looking for anything I might have overlooked. Satisfied that I was prepared to follow Harvey Kahill, I headed back to my apartment.

Driving gives a man time to think—sometimes too much time. My idle thoughts drifted to Molly and that wretched day and what my life had become since. I was on the Seward Highway, slowing for a red light at Northern Lights Boulevard, when, on an impulse, I jerked the wheel to the left and pointed the car westbound, toward one of the more affluent parts of the city. Five minutes later I hooked a left and then a right and another left and pulled to the curb in front of a handsome two-story brick dwelling with forest-green shutters and a manicured lawn. I slumped down in my seat and stared at the front door zombie-like. After a while a heard a soft patter on the windshield. I sat listening to the rain tap out a slow and steady rhythm.

A weary smile curled my lips. How long had it been? Nine, ten years? And yet, in my mind's eye, I saw her sitting next to me like it was yesterday. She was beaming when she turned to me and said, "I love it."

"Really?" I replied. "You haven't even seen the inside."

"Sometimes you just know."

"How do you know?"

"I have a feeling."

"You have a feeling."

"Haven't you ever just had a feeling?"

I didn't answer.

She said, "This is the one."

"Don't you want to know if the washer and dryer work? Or the dishwasher? What about a workbench?"

"That's just stuff. Look at this place! I love the trees. And that big brass doorknocker. It feels right to me."

I just stared at her and sighed. "Okay, but can I at least have a peek inside the garage?"

She hugged me until my neck hurt. "You won't regret this."

A sharp rap on the window brought me back to the present. I peered through the rain-dappled window at a broad-shouldered man with a thick crop of black hair wearing gray sweatpants and a matching sweatshirt. He motioned for me to roll down the window. I did.

A thin, straight line of a mouth opened. "You lost, pal?"

"No, I just—"

"Waiting for someone?"

"I . . . I used to live here."

It didn't register at first, but then he took a step back as if struck by a blast of hot air. "Say, aren't you the husband of that woman who . . . damn. Look, mister, I'm sorry. You can sit here if you want. You know, we've got this Neighborhood Watch group and, well, we like to . . ."

I held up a hand. "It's okay. I was just leaving."

I heard him say, "Hey, pal, are you okay?" as the Subaru inched away from the curb. When I glanced at the rearview mirror, he was still standing there in the rain, watching me.

Four

I dragged myself out of bed shortly after ten Friday morning wearing a hangover from the Prospector Bar, but a long, hot shower and a couple of aspirin returned me to a state of relative normalcy. Normalcy for me, at least. I skipped coffee at the Mighty Moose, wishing to avoid the inevitable rebuke from Rachel, and hoofed it three blocks to the Downtown Deli, where I wolfed down the Breakfast Combo, paying the waitress out of Elizabeth Landers' retainer.

My appetite sated, I slow-walked the streets of downtown Anchorage. Yesterday's precipitation had left puddles on the sidewalks, fresh termination dust on the mountains, and the air crisp and sweet, with pillowy clouds giving way to flashes of midday sunshine. The streets were filled with people smiling and chatting as though everything was all right.

My impromptu visit to the old house had triggered memories I'd struggled to keep buried since last December. Memories of a time when everything seemed to be in its proper place. When *I* was all right.

It was almost 2 p.m. when my wanderings brought me back to my apartment. Priscilla glanced up from Molly's rocker and yawned. I tossed my coat on the couch and shagged a beer from the fridge before sprawling out on the couch with the legal pad filled with Elizabeth Lander's notes.

It's impossible to over-prepare for surveillance. Once the show starts there's no time to pull over to the side of the road and check your notes. One hour and three beers later, I tossed the pad on the coffee table and leaned back to rest my eyes. When I opened them again a glance at my watch told me it was 5:30.

I'd slept for two hours. I donned a jacket, picked up my cheat sheet and photo of Harvey, and headed out the door. It was clear and cold. I walked briskly to the parking garage, cursing myself for not bringing a heavier jacket.

Don't fuck this up.

The drive to the Hillside was uneventful. At half past six, I maneuvered snugly into the spot I'd picked out during my earlier reconnaissance. Based on what Elizabeth had told me, she and Harvey would be having dinner about now. I settled in for what I hoped would be a brief wait.

Harvey didn't disappoint. His gray Tundra emerged from the garage at four minutes past seven. Thirty seconds later the big truck cruised past me at an easy pace. I allowed him a hundred-yard lead and slipped in behind him. He kept his eyes locked on the road ahead, averting his gaze only when the necessities of driving required it. By all indications, Harvey was going to be an easy tail.

I learned the craft of surveillance while serving in the Army Criminal Investigation Division—CID. I'd enlisted right out of high school after seeing how dim my prospects were of finding work in my hometown back in Ohio. I loved being an Army cop so much that I made a twenty-year career out of it, including three tours in Germany. When the time came for reassignment I was offered a choice gig in Alaska and jumped on it with both feet. I thought Molly would be happy here. Apparently I was wrong.

Harvey led me off the Hillside, his pace unwavering. If we stayed on course, in five minutes we'd come to the Seward Highway, the primary north-south artery through Anchorage. Turn north and you're headed downtown. Follow it south and you're on your way to Girdwood and, eventually, the Kenai Peninsula.

I love the feel of the open road. The freedom that comes with not knowing what lies ahead. I think it's why I like surveillance work so much. You never know quite what to expect.

As we approached the Seward Highway on-ramp, I assumed Harvey would turn north toward downtown Anchorage. It seemed logical, after all. Why turn south?

Well, I was wrong. He turned south.

What are you up to, Harvey?

We were on the south edge of town and darkness was fast approaching. There was nothing in that direction for forty miles except roads, mountains, water, and a few scattered dwellings. If he were intending to meet someone, why come all the way out here?

We bid farewell to Anchorage, descending onto a two-lane straightaway. To my left, Potter's Marsh was ablaze in fiery red hues, a gift from the evening sun. A trio of Trumpeter swans circled for a landing. To my right, the waters of Cook Inlet were hidden from view by the raised bed of the Alaska Railroad, but I could still see the snow-capped mountains in the distance. Beyond those tracks, the exposed tidal flats skirted the broad, watery inlet known as Turnagain Arm. When the tide is in, windsurfers can sometimes be seen darting around like human sailboats.

Past Potter's Marsh the highway lifted and the full splendor of Turnagain Arm revealed itself. Molly had loved driving along the Arm, although as my P.I. business consumed increasing amounts of my time, our drives had become less frequent.

The marshy area on my left gave way to a steep mountain face that continued for many miles. Rivulets of icy water kissed the walls of gray rock. I scouted the rocky outcroppings for the sure-footed Dall sheep that roamed these cliffs and sometimes ventured onto the highway below, but today I saw none. A semi whooshed by heading north, rocking the Subaru and reminding me to keep both eyes focused on the narrow, winding road.

Five minutes later the Tundra abruptly swung left into a large parking area terraced into the side of the mountain. I knew this place. It was the McHugh Creek Trailhead, part of the vast Chugach State Park. Molly and I used to come here to hike and pick blueberries. I cruised past the entrance a couple of hundred feet, hooked a U-turn, and pulled to the side of the road. I watched as Harvey zigzagged through the parking area, working his way up the hill. He passed an old red short-bed pickup parked midway up the hill, ignoring its presence. When he reached the upper level, he pulled to a stop with the Tundra facing away from the highway.

I pulled back onto the highway, hung a right into the parking lot, and cruised slowly down the first row, all the while keeping the Tundra in sight. Near the end of the row, I lucked out and found a parking place hidden from Harvey's field of view. If he walked down the hill he'd see my car, but hopefully he'd think I was just another hiker out for a late evening stroll.

I shut off the Subaru, grabbed my binoculars from under the seat, and started up the hill. Hugging the rocky slope bordering the left side of the parking area, I was able to keep Harvey's truck in sight most of the time while remaining relatively hidden.

A few minutes of uphill hiking was enough to convince me I was seriously out of shape. I'd been an active man in my youth, and Molly kept me in shape with frequent hikes and sparring sessions on the tennis court. But with months of apathy and twenty pounds of beer gut under my belt, I found myself huffing and puffing like an old geezer. I made a mental note to get back in shape. I figured I could do that on Saturday since I didn't have anything else on my calendar.

After five minutes of rigorous climbing, the ground leveled off. Although I couldn't see it, I guessed I was roughly even with the Tundra and turned south along the ridge. I'd gone about a hundred feet when the truck came into view. I ducked down behind a boulder roughly the size of a sea turtle and peered over it. The Tundra stood at the edge of the paved parking area some ninety feet away. Beyond it, concealed by thick woods, was the McHugh Creek Trailhead.

Had Harvey gone up the trail or was he still in his truck?

I looked around for a better observation post, but there was nothing but trees and small rocks. The boulder would have to do. I scraped away loose brush and stones as best I could, eased into a prone position on the ground, and trained my binoculars on the Tundra. Harvey was behind the wheel, staring through the windshield. He was alone. I scanned the area in all directions but saw no one. I glanced at my watch and noted the time: 7:52.

The minutes ticked by, the dampness of the evening air seeping into my bones like an unwelcome intruder. I longed for the warmth of my apartment. What was Harvey doing here? Meeting someone? If so, who? A lover? A drug connection?

A flash of movement caught my eye. The Tundra's door sprang open. Harvey eased himself out of the cab, looked around furtively, and began pacing the blacktop around the truck. The upper half of his body filled the circular limits of the binoculars' vision and I saw his face clearly for the first time. It held a look of impending doom.

What have you gotten yourself into, Harvey?

He paced in an oddly repetitive way, like bears do when they've been caged for a long period of time. After several minutes of this, it dawned on me that the binoculars' high power limited my field of view, forcing me to focus all of my attention on his face. The detective in me whispered: Don't do that.

I lowered the binoculars and allowed my eyes a chance to rest. Off to the west, the receding light of evening cast an eerie glow over the tidal flats far, far below. The air was deathly still, the only sound the occasional car or truck on the highway and the mournful cackle of a passing raven. The red truck I had noticed earlier had departed.

I brought the binoculars back to eye level. My quarry was hard to find through the brush and gloom—it was getting dark and fast. When I finally had him in my sights he was still pacing, but now his arms were no longer at his sides. They were out in front of him and he was holding something. A cell phone, perhaps? I couldn't be sure.

Turn around. Let's see what you've got in your hands, buddy.

As if in response, Harvey turned around. Straining my eyes, I followed his right arm down to his hands and saw . . . a dark blob. Damn. The object, whatever it was, blended perfectly with his dark clothing. He turned again, showing me his backside.

My body involuntarily shook from the cold penetrating my clothing and in another ten or fifteen minutes it would be difficult to see my own hands, let alone his.

Another thought occurred to me: If Harvey decided to hop in his truck and drive off, I'd be left scurrying over rocky terrain in the dark. I hoped that whatever was going to happen happened soon.

The very instant that thought coursed through my brain, Harvey turned back toward me. A glint of dusky light and some beveled lines quickly morphed into a more distinct shape—one I knew all too well.

Harvey Kahill's pale hands held the cold, blue steel of a revolver.

A chill penetrated my already chilled body. Should I confront him? Call 911? As I contemplated my next move, Harvey stood there with the gun in his hands, massaging it, almost caressing it. A knot swelled in the pit of my stomach. My heart pounded in my chest like a jackhammer. My hands shook from the cold and my own pumping adrenalin. I wished I'd remembered my Ruger, tucked neatly under the front seat of the Subaru.

I raised the binoculars and watched in horror as Harvey cocked his elbow and stuck the gun barrel in his mouth.

Sweet Jesus.

I struggled to rise, but my forty-five-year-old legs, numb with cold, were like anchors holding me down. My feet pumped wildly, kicking up loose gravel as I fought to gain traction. With agonizing slowness I picked up speed until, at a dead run, with my arms flailing wildly, I screamed "Noooo!" at the top of my lungs. My pitiful wail evaporated in a sickening crack of gunfire as Harvey's head exploded in a plume of crimson mist.

Five

It was close to midnight at the McHugh Creek Trailhead. Harvey Kahill had been dead for several hours, and I was none too lively myself. The several hours I'd spent standing in that parking lot answering questions and waiting around had taken a toll on my nerves and my patience. I was cold, hungry, and dog-tired.

A dozen yards away, Barney Pendleton, chief investigator with the Alaska State Troopers, scratched his balding head for what must have been the tenth time as he leaned against the open door of his unmarked car and chatted with a pair of uniformed officers. Pendleton was there to investigate Harvey's death, which was unfortunate for me because the two of us shared an unpleasant history.

On the far side of the Tundra, two paramedics hovered over Harvey's body, presumably waiting for an investigator from the medical examiner's office to release the body so they could transport it to the state crime lab for an autopsy. Several other troopers were walking around, the chalky white beams of their flashlights stabbing the night air. The squawk and chatter of police radios echoed off the surrounding mountains. As I stood beside the Subaru, stomping my feet for warmth and watching the eerie scene, I replayed in my head the events of the evening, events that had turned my routine surveillance into a living nightmare.

Nothing in this life quite prepares you for the sight of a man shooting himself in the head. For me, at least, it helped somehow to break it down into logical parts, like a schematic. As the bullet tore through Harvey's brain at over one thousand feet per second, the missile's kinetic energy and the hydrostatic shock wave it created caused his head to expand at an enormous rate and to quite literally explode before my eyes. In less than a millisecond his ravaged brain stopped transmitting signals to the spinal cord, instantly halting all motor activity. Result: Harvey dropped to the ground like a 200-pound sack of rice. Not at all like it happens in the movies.

I don't know how long I stood there—adrenalin plays tricks on one's sense of time—but in due course, I walked over to the truck, dug into my pocket for my flashlight, and thumbed it on. Harvey's legs were akimbo, his body strangely twisted. He lay on his left side, left arm beneath him. His right hand still held the gun, fingers clutching the pistol grip in a peculiar form of muscle stiffening the lab boys call cadaveric spasm, a phenomenon common with self-inflicted gunshot wounds.

The gun was a .357 magnum Smith & Wesson revolver with a four-inch barrel, and the wound it produced was frightening. The back of Harvey's head was gone, the resulting cavity rimmed with soaked and matted hair. Blood oozed from the wound, steam rising from the warm fluid. On the pavement behind the body, flecks of blood and brain matter glowed cherry red under the flashlight's cold white beam. I shined it next on his face. His eyes were wide and frozen in classic deer-in-the-headlights fashion. A narrow river of blood flowed from between slightly parted lips.

I stood and took a step back. It was all too weird and all too real at the same time. I felt a dark force pull me back to an eerily similar scene not so long ago. I fought to sweep that image from my mind, with only partial success.

Turning away, I walked the few steps to the Tundra, stuck my head through the half-opened door, and panned my light around the interior. It was immaculate. Harvey kept a clean vehicle. I was about to pull my head out of the cab when a flash of white drew my attention to the center console. There, wedged inside a cup holder, was a folded-up piece of paper. I leaned across the seat and snatched it up. A half-sheet of white paper bore a note handwritten in blue ink: Harvey's suicide note. I read it quickly, stuffed it in my shirt, and then fished around in my coat pocket for my cell phone.

My first instinct had been to drive out of there and find a pay phone, place an anonymous call to the 911 operator, and report that while hiking at McHugh Creek I had happened upon the body of a man lying dead in the parking lot near a pickup truck. I'd then hang up and walk away from the phone. Had I done that I wouldn't have been freezing my bunions off in the middle of the night, having to deal with Pendleton. But I realized there were a whole lot of things that could go wrong with that course of action, not least of which was my being accused of murder later on. So, unappealing as the prospect was, I dialed 911, gave the operator my name, and told her what I had witnessed.

The call I made to my client was, by comparison, much worse. She picked up on the first ring.

"Hello?" Her voice was filled with both anticipation and dread.

"Elizabeth. It's Sidney."

"Hello, Sidney. Do you have something to report?"

I really hate this.

As advanced as we are as a civilization, no one has yet discovered a good way to deliver bad news. "I think you should sit down."

Her voice tensed. "Oh, God. What has he done?"

I could have let the troopers do this. After all, it's their job to notify next of kin. Technically, she wasn't even my client anymore. The assignment was over.

"I followed him south on the Seward Highway. He pulled into the McHugh Rec Area, where he . . . dang it, there's no easy way to say it. Harvey shot himself, Elizabeth. He's . . . he's dead. I'm sorry."

There was a sharp gasp. "Sidney . . . how?"

"That's really all I know. Look, I have to go. The troopers will be here any minute. I'm so sorry."

As I ended the connection, what I thought was the sound of Elizabeth sobbing on the other end of the line was instead the distant wail of sirens headed south from Anchorage.

The paramedics arrived first, sirens blaring. After chatting with them briefly, I walked down to my car and moved it closer to the scene. Then I waited for the rest of the cavalry. Pendleton pulled up, greeting me with an icy stare. "So it was you who called. What brought you all the way out here, another one of your hunches?"

I occupy a revered place on Pendleton's shit list. Cops do not generally hold P.I.'s in very high esteem in any case—which I find ironic, considering they all want to be private eyes when they retire—but the animus between us was particularly intense. My work as a defense investigator had placed me on the opposite side of the courtroom podium on more than one occasion, and in one particular case my sworn testimony had contradicted his. Then there was another time I'd given him a tip—a tip he'd acted on and which had left him substantially embarrassed. He never forgave me for it.

"Nice to see you, too, Officer Pendleton. I hope I haven't taken you away from anything important."

"Enough with the wisecracks, Reed. Just tell me what happened."

I gave him the short version. When I'd finished there was silence as he scribbled away in his notebook. Then he looked up at me. "Who hired you?"

I bristled at the question. Confidentiality is part of a P.I.'s stock in trade. I said nothing.

His words rang cold. "I have to be able to verify your story, so tell me the goddamn name or I'll arrest you for interfering with my investigation."

I told him. Sure, I could have acted all pious and let him arrest me, but in the end I would have been dragged in front of a judge and ordered to give it up anyway. It didn't seem like a good use of my time. And Priscilla would miss me.

Pendleton wrote down Elizabeth's name and phone number and told me to go wait by my car like a good little P.I. Then he drove up to the Tundra and did investigator stuff while I milled about near the now-cordoned-off scene.

In due course, more officers arrived, among them a fair-haired, fortyish woman carrying a black kit bag. It was Lois Dosier, an investigator with the medical examiner's office. She glanced in my direction and waved in recognition. After chatting briefly with the paramedics, she crouched over the body and went to work—a poke here, a prod there—all the while filling out various forms. Finally, she took a series of photographs of the prone figure, the camera flashes illuminating the night like tiny bolts of lightning.

The investigators are the unsung heroes of the medical examiner's office. Upon notification of a death anywhere within Alaska's far-flung borders, they pack their bags and go—come rain, shine, or waist-deep snow.

Lois and I go back to my Army days. When I first met her, she was a staff sergeant in a military police battalion in Germany. While working together on a major drug case we became friends. On my recommendation, she joined the CID and made a career of it, as I had done. We kept in touch through the years. She'd always been an avid hiker and parasailing enthusiast, so when she retired she didn't need much encouragement to follow Molly and me to Alaska. She had hired on with the M.E.'s office six years ago.

While Lois was completing her work Pendleton walked over and spoke to her, his gestures betraying his frustration. Minutes later he stalked away and Lois, flashlight in hand, strode over to me. "I'm afraid Pendleton doesn't like you very much."

"Pendleton doesn't like anyone smarter than he is. Which is to say, he doesn't like anyone."

She shot me a concerned look. "Watch yourself, Sid. He can make your life a living hell."

"It already is." I shuffled my feet. "How have you been, Lois?"

"Livin' the dream. How are you, my friend?"

I lowered my head, avoiding her gaze. "I've been better."

In the days and weeks following Molly's death, Lois had tried to reach me, but I was in no mood for human contact, preferring the contents of a Corona bottle.

She looked at me in the dim light. "Sid, I . . ."

"What do you say we get this done so we can all go home?" I gave her the same short version I gave Pendleton.

She wrote it down and sighed. "I inspected the body and truck. Looks like suicide to me. I don't expect anything different from the autopsy." We walked slowly through the night in the direction of her car, her flashlight lighting the way. "Pendleton's not happy about this. He doesn't think it adds up, you watching this guy at the same time he decides to blow his brains out. He thinks it's suspicious." She stopped. "I say, tough shit. I don't work for him."

"Thanks, Lois."

We looked at each other. Her face was all shadows from the flashlight. She said, "I'm sorry about Molly."

I dug at the ground with my boot.

She kept looking at me like she was staring down a gun sight. I knew I wasn't going to get away, not from her, so I let go and we hugged and tears rolled down my cheeks in the chill night air. The only sound was our own breathing and the dull chatter of voices up the hill. We walked to her car and she turned to me.

"I'm glad you're working again, though I'm guessing this wasn't the outcome you had in mind. You know, you can't hide forever." Lois slid behind the wheel and started the engine. She leaned her head out the window. "It's about time we played chess again, don't you think? Or are you afraid of getting your ass beat?"

That coaxed the makings of a smile out of me. I watched her car wind its way out of the parking lot and turn north on the Seward Highway. Beyond the highway to the west, moonlight shimmered across the inlet, the ghostly light dancing atop the waves. If those rollers made any noise I couldn't hear it above the idling engines of the trooper cars still on the scene.

I walked to my car and fired up the engine. One by one the remaining officers left McHugh Creek, their flashlight beams flittering like fireflies as they headed back to their vehicles and drove away. The last one to leave pulled up beside me. Pendleton stuck his light in my face. "Okay, Reed," he said gruffly. "I don't need you anymore. Not tonight, anyway."

"Swell."

"One more thing." He stared at me like he'd been taught in trooper school. Or was it reform school? "Don't go anywhere. I may need to ask you some more questions."

I watched his red taillights disappear from view, then switched off the engine. I don't know how long I sat there before falling asleep. When I woke, a sheen of frost coated the windshield.

Six

I shoved open the door to my apartment a bit shy of 2 a.m., made a beeline for the kitchen, and opened the fridge. No beer. I dug around and found an old bottle of Merlot. Three-quarters of it was gone. I carried the bottle into the living room and flopped on the couch. Priscilla jumped off the rocker and pounced on my lap.

The accumulated stress of the evening engulfed me. I lifted the bottle and drank. How long since I'd opened it? Three, maybe four months? I took another long swig and then another. In due course, I felt an all-too-familiar buzz. When the bottle was empty I set it on the coffee table, stretched out on the couch, and pressed my eyelids together.

On a perfect Sunday afternoon, Molly and I stride briskly along our favorite hiking trail, holding hands as we go. Above us, a canopy of lush green gives way to radiant blue sky. We glance at each other and smile, reveling in the beauty that surrounds us. An hour later we arrive back at the trailhead and slow to an easy walk, letting the sun warm our faces. As we approach the Subaru I notice a black pickup in the adjacent space. A man sits behind the wheel. Devoid of facial features, he is oddly white and lifeless. I look around for other cars, but there are none. He steps out of his vehicle and stands by the door, motionless. I step closer and he opens his mouth to speak.

"This is your lucky day, Mr. Reed."

Then, as calmly as if he were folding a newspaper, he sticks a pistol in his mouth. Instantly his head explodes. Blood and gore fly in every direction. I turn to check on Molly, but my muscles are rubbery and unresponsive. When I speak the words trickle out. "Molly, did you see . . ." I stare in disbelief. No longer wearing her trademark pink sweats and headband, she is clad in white from head to toe—her wedding dress. She has never looked more beautiful. I lower my gaze to her hands. To my horror, they grip a pistol. The one I bought her. The one she hates so much. I want to ask her why, but before I can find the words she looks at me calmly and says, "He's right, Sidney. This is your lucky day." Slowly she brings the gun to her head.

I sprang bolt upright, bathed in a cold sweat, my heart pounding in my chest. I gulped deep breaths of life-giving air until my mind began to focus. The same dream I'd been having since her death had returned with a vengeance, only this time Harvey Kahill had joined the show.

My watch told me it was 9:45 a.m. Priscilla sidled up next to me. Once my heart rate had slowed to a respectable seventy beats per minute I eased myself into a standing position. My legs shook like corn stalks in a summer storm. When the shaking stopped I started for the fridge to grab a beer, then remembered that I'd run out.

I threw on sweats and drove to the local stop-and-rob to stock up on Corona and other needed supplies. I came back and spent the remainder of Saturday on the couch with Priscilla, drinking beer and watching classic Sherlock Holmes movies—the good ones, starring Basil Rathbone as the great detective. I passed out halfway through *The Woman In Green*.

I awakened late Sunday morning with a pounding headache and a craving for the company of humans. I headed downstairs, where Rachel Saint George eyed me with a mixture of playfulness and concern.

"Well, it's about time. I was starting to worry about you." She glanced over me with a smirk. "By the way, nice outfit."

Following her gaze, I glanced down: I was wearing my bathrobe and slippers. When I looked up, half a dozen patrons were staring at me. A few smiled. One woman giggled. I said, "Oops."

"This is a coffee shop, not the Playboy Mansion," Rachel said with mock sternness, adding for good measure, "and you're definitely not Hugh Hefner."

"Yeah, well, you're not Miss September."

"Ass." She took my order—coffee, black. Glancing furtively around the shop, she leaned across the counter. "Sidney, are you all right?"

I decided not to tell her about my Friday night ordeal. "I'm fine."

"Oh, really? Well, it didn't seem that way yesterday. In fact, I almost called the cops."

"What are you talking about?"

"I got worried when you didn't come down so I banged on your door late last evening and got no response. Nothing. Nada. I thought maybe you were dead."

"I was. What time were you banging?"

"Six-thirty or thereabouts."

"I must have been asleep. What gives?"

"A reporter lady came by looking for you. Perky little thing."

"Did she say what she wanted?"

"No, and I didn't ask. What you do up in that apartment is none of my business."

"Don't worry, I stopped sacrificing virgins months ago."

Rachel grinned playfully.

I said, "What else did she say?"

"She asked me to tell you she had been by and to give her a call."

"What could she possibly want from me?" I said, scratching the stubble on my chin.

"Why don't you ask her yourself?" She handed me a white business card that read *Anchorage Daily News* in burgundy lettering across the middle. In the upper right-hand corner, in smaller black lettering, were the words: *Maria Maldonado, News Reporter.*

"Nice name," I said, stuffing the card in the pocket of my bathrobe. "I like her already."

"That's because you're a man. Her name could be Mandy Mudd and you'd still like her."

"Good point."

She slid an empty mug across the counter and I filled it from a silver thermos labeled "House Brew" on a side table. On the way out the door I spotted a copy of the Sunday paper on a table. I grabbed it and lumbered back upstairs, where I spent the next two hours vegging. At some point I remembered I hadn't seen my cell phone in two days. I searched the usual spots—coffee table, nightstand, wastebasket—but came up empty-handed. I got down on my hands and knees and found it on the floor between the couch and end table. Easing into the couch, I powered it up and noticed one missed call. I played back the message.

"Sid, Lois. Call me." I dialed her cell. She picked up on the first ring.

"Hey, Sid, what took you so long?" she demanded before I had a chance to say anything. "I've got the Kahill autopsy results. Thought you should know before it hit the papers."

"That was quick."

"What can I say? Business has been slow."

"Don't you mean dead?"

"Not funny."

"It was a little funny."

"You want the results or not?"

"Shoot. I can take it."

"Now that *was* funny. Okay, let's see here. Oh yeah. Cause of death: single gunshot wound to the head. Manner of death: suicide. No indication of foul play."

I managed, "That's great news, thanks."

"Try to contain your enthusiasm."

I didn't reply.

"Hey, bud, you all right?"

"I'm fine. Still a little shook up, that's all."

"Can't say I blame you. Witnessing something like that after what happened to Molly . . ." Her voice trailed off. "Well," she said at last, "if you need to talk, you know how to reach me."

I hung up the phone. Lois was a dear friend and she meant well, but I didn't really need to be reminded about what happened to Molly—the nightmares were serving that purpose quite well.

I picked up the paper and scanned the news. I spotted Harvey's obit in the middle of Section B. There was a short blurb about his fairly short life, love of hunting, successful business, blah, blah, blah. No mention of suicide or where he'd been found. The last sentence said funeral services were scheduled for Tuesday at the Midnight Sun Funeral Home, which happened to be located downtown, not far from my apartment.

My thoughts turned to Elizabeth. I hadn't spoken to her since the night Harvey died. Not that I'd expected her to call me. She had a lot on her plate right now. And then I remembered the suicide note.

I thought for a moment and then made a beeline for the dirty clothes pile where, after some digging, I found the shirt I'd worn that day. The note was in the vest pocket where I'd left it. Returning to the couch, I read Harvey's last words:

Dearest Elizabeth—
I never thought it would come to this but here I am. You can outrun the past only so long before it catches up to you. Please leave Alaska now—there's nothing for you here. You will find my last will in the safe with my other papers. There is enough to start a new life Outside. Not that you need it. Know that I never meant to hurt you. I only wish there was another way. Please don't hate me. I love you. Harvey

A hundred questions came to mind, but I didn't want to hear them. The guy asking those questions—Sidney Reed, P.I.—had retreated safely to his corner and, if I had anything to say about it, would stay there. Whatever Harvey's demons may have been, he had dispatched them handily with a single gunshot to the head. As for my client, her inquiry had ended with Harvey's death. Case closed.

Pendleton would shit a brick if he knew I'd taken the note, and then he'd arrest me for tampering with evidence. I didn't much care. If I gave it to him it would only end up locked away in the evidence room at APD. Screw that.

I decided to attend Harvey's funeral on Tuesday, hand Elizabeth the note, wish her a happy life, and get the hell out of there. In the meantime, I had a bookcase full of Sherlock Holmes movies and a fridge stocked with Corona. I stuffed the note into my bathrobe pocket. My fingers bumped into the business card Rachel had given me, the one left by the reporter. I could only think of one reason a reporter would be calling me now. She wanted to ask about McHugh Creek. Nothing good could come of that.

I tossed the card in the trash on my way to the fridge.

Seven

I hate funerals. The last one I had attended was Molly's. After it was all over I had gone home and thrown up in the john. The worst thing about throwing up is the nasty aftertaste. Now, as I walked into the Midnight Sun Funeral Home, I could feel that taste welling up in my throat.

The place was packed with mourners, some standing alone or in small groups, others seated in padded stackable chairs arranged neatly in rows facing a lectern. Behind it, a gilded bronze coffin draped in purple velvet held the body of Harvey Kahill. The lid was closed. A good embalmer can only do so much.

Scanning the sea of faces left little doubt that Harvey had been a well-respected member of the Anchorage business community. I recognized a city councilman, the deputy police chief, and the president of the Chamber of Commerce.

Scanning further, my roving eyes landed on a huge man seated in the first row. He was perhaps forty years old and topped with a wisp of thinning light brown hair. He had a square-jawed and weathered look that reminded me of the western film star, Gary Cooper. Being a head taller than anyone else there, he stood out from the crowd—literally. As I was musing on his size, he turned to his left and spoke to an attractive blonde in a black dress whom I immediately recognized as Elizabeth Landers.

Just then a rather stiff, partly balding man intoned all those present to be seated, so I grabbed a chair in the back row. It was a pleasant service, as funerals go. One by one, mourners stood to say nice things about Harvey, but then no one has anything bad to say at a funeral. I was reminded of a line from a John Lennon tune: *Everybody loves you when you're six feet in the ground.*

After some remarks by Reverend What's-his-name, an organ began piping out a funeral dirge, signaling the close of the service. The mourners rose and shuffled single file past a grieving Elizabeth, paying their respects with soft-voiced condolences, the patting of hands, and the dabbing away of tears. Off to her side and slightly behind her, the big man I'd seen earlier was talking to her. Poised and polite, Elizabeth was attempting to listen to him while accepting the condolences of the mourners. Once the line of well-wishers had subsided, I approached her, offering my hand. "I'm so sorry for your loss."

She clasped her hands around mine. "Thank you for coming, Sidney." The strain and grief etched into her tired eyes spoke volumes. She withdrew her hand and turned to the hulking giant hovering nearby. He moved closer.

"Joe, I want you to meet someone. This is Sidney Reed. Sidney, Joe Meacham, an old and dear friend of mine."

I recalled from Elizabeth's notes and our earlier conversation that Joe was the third "Amigo"—the last surviving member of Harvey's inner circle and the man who killed the moose that killed Tom Landers. We shook hands and I winced. My grip is not weak, but his felt like the squeeze of a bench vise. I wondered if he shook hands like that with everyone or if his display of strength was for my benefit. I'm suspicious that way.

He said, "Any friend of Elizabeth is a friend of mine."

I was pretty sure he didn't mean it, but I always try to be polite at funerals, so I said, "Likewise."

Harvey's suicide note was burning a hole in my pocket, but I decided against handing it to her inside the funeral home, choosing instead to take her aside once we'd exited the building.

The crowd had begun to surge toward the door as Elizabeth turned to speak with someone, so I decided to head outside. Falling in line behind Meacham as he strode toward the door, I felt a tug at my sleeve and stopped. Elizabeth pulled me aside. "Excuse me, Sidney. I know this is short notice, but will you come to my house later this afternoon? I have some business I need to discuss with you."

Out of the corner of my eye, I saw Joe glance over his shoulder at us before shuffling out the door. Turning to Elizabeth, I looked into those soft blue eyes and saw that same urgency and strength I had witnessed when she stood in my apartment. My instincts told me to say no.

What could she possibly want from me now?

I glanced at the casket, then back at Elizabeth. She was still looking at me. This woman wasn't used to being told no.

"All right," I said without much enthusiasm. "I'll be there."

"Good."

We arrived at the door and I held it open as she passed through. Joe was waiting, somewhat impatiently, a short distance away. When she reached him, they walked side by side to a late-model Mercedes parked at the front of the motorcade. Joe held the passenger door open as she got in and then walked around to the driver's side and slid behind the wheel.

I turned toward the parking lot, having decided to skip the burial, and hadn't gone twenty paces when I saw a young woman walking briskly toward me. I guessed her to be between thirty and thirty-five years old, five-three or so, and thin, with a smallish frame. Long, dark brown hair was pulled back in a ponytail and she wore a red and green plaid shirt, corduroy slacks, hiking boots, and an old brown coat that looked more like a throw rug. Her gate was quick and purposeful.

"Sidney Reed? I'm Maria Maldonado, reporter with the Anchorage Daily News."

The reporter who left the business card. Damn.

"What can I do for you, Miss Maldonado?" I made no attempt to conceal my irritation.

"I'd like to talk to you about the death of Harvey Kahill."

She said it loud enough that several of the mourners milling around glanced in our direction.

"No comment." I started to walk away, but she was on me like a bottle-nose fly on a picnic basket.

"Mr. Reed, I understand you were present when Mr. Kahill committed suicide. What can you tell me about that?"

She stepped in front of me, but I deftly pushed past her. "Go Away. Shoo." I kept walking. She followed.

"Please, Mr. Reed. If I could have just a minute of your time."

I didn't want her following me home so I stopped.

Maybe I can finesse my way out of this.

I said, "All right, you have one minute."

She looked right at me with intelligent, probing eyes. "What were you doing at McHugh Creek last Friday night?"

"I was bird watching."

Sidney, you're pathetic.

"Come on, Mr. Reed. You can do better than that."

Her hair was the color of chestnuts. I love chestnuts, but I still had no intention of telling her my business. "You're one minute is up, Miss Maldonado. Have a nice day."

As I was walked away I got hit with a big fat curveball.

"Is there any truth to the rumor that Kahill was murdered?"

I froze in my tracks.

Harvey Kahill murdered? Where did that come from?

I turned to face her. "Where on earth did you—"

She'd pulled a digital recorder from her coat pocket and held it out in front of her. "Well, Mr. Reed?"

I said, "Oh, I get it. This is where I lose my cool and babble something titillating for your readers, right? Forget it, that's not going to happen."

Her face went blank and the arm holding the recorder dropped to her side. "No, Mr. Reed. This is where you tell me the truth."

I tried to think of a snappy comeback. Nothing came.

Who is this woman?

Finally, I said, "I'm sorry but there's nothing I can tell you."

She tucked the recorder in her coat pocket. "Mr. Reed, I have better things to do with my time than bat my eyes like some airhead from a supermarket tabloid. I'm a journalist. Have a nice day."

With that, she turned and walked away.

Sidney, my boy, you sure know how to finesse the ladies.

Eight

Elizabeth Landers' living room was tastefully decorated, luxurious in its appointments, and huge—my entire apartment would have fit inside it with room to spare. And then there was the fireplace: a great granite edifice dominating one wall. It was hard not to be impressed.

"Please have a seat, Sidney. May I pour you a drink?"

She stood in the middle of the room, still wearing the black dress from the funeral, the strain of the last few days etched on her face. Even so, she remained composed, professional—in control.

"Beer, if it's not too much trouble."

"I have Bitter Monk IPA and Alaskan Amber."

"Amber will be fine." I eased into a blue lavender sofa. She strode into the kitchen and I heard the fridge open and the crisp clink of glass. Moments later she returned carrying a beer bottle and a glass of wine.

"Harvey was a beer lover," she said, "although I never cared for it myself. Give me champagne or a nice chardonnay any day."

Just give me something alcoholic.

She handed me the ice-cold bottle, settled in opposite me in a matching blue lavender chair, and sipped some wine. I lifted the bottle to my lips and heard her sigh.

"I still can't believe he's gone," she said, staring past me.

I followed her gaze out through an expansive picture window that offered a commanding view of Cook Inlet. The cold blue water shimmered under an afternoon sky that glowed pink and purple.

"Beautiful, isn't it?"

"Yes," I agreed, glancing around the room. "And this house is amazing."

She beamed with unmistakable affection. "You're looking at Tom Landers' legacy. We had planned to grow old here together." Her brow creased in sorrow. "Unfortunately, our lives don't always turn out the way we intend."

Ain't that the truth.

She sipped wine and stared longingly out the window.

I shifted uncomfortably in my seat. "With all due respect, Elizabeth, why am I here?"

She put down her glass, sat up ramrod straight, and looked at me. "I have another job for you. I want you to find out why Harvey killed himself."

I stared at her in disbelief. "Listen, I know how painful this must be for you. You want to make sense of it, to find answers—"

"Don't patronize me, Sidney. That's really the last thing I need right now." She rose to her feet. "Come, let me show you something."

I set my beer next to her wine and followed her to the fireplace. Ever so gently she lifted a framed photograph from the long oak mantel and handed it to me. "Look at this and tell me what you see."

It was a photograph of a much younger Elizabeth and Harvey standing side by side in a warm embrace on a lush, grassy slope. There were snow-capped mountains behind them. "Happy couple," I said, and handed it back. "When was it taken?"

"Twenty years ago. The year we graduated from McKinley. So you see, he's not someone I just jumped into bed with after Tom died. He was a dear, dear friend. And at the risk of tooting my own horn, he was grateful beyond words to have me in his life. The point being, I know Harvey. He was not the sort of man who would take his own life. On the contrary, he had everything to live for."

I patted my breast pocket containing the suicide note,

wondering if this was the right time to show her. As if there could ever be a right time.

She returned the photograph to the mantel. "Harvey and I were to be married this Christmas. We were a week away from making the announcement." She was close to tears but fought them off. "Would you excuse me for a moment?" She walked smartly to the kitchen and rummaged through her red handbag until she found what she was looking for. She came back and handed me a slip of blue paper.

I stared at it numbly. It was a check for five thousand dollars. I looked at her, searching for something to say.

"I assure you, there is more where that came from."

"Elizabeth, I . . . I can't accept this."

"Of course you can." Her eyes were piercing, her jaw set. "You're an investigator. Investigate."

"I can't. There would be no point to it."

"You don't believe that."

She was right. Alarm bells were ringing up and down the halls of my investigator's brain: Harvey's suicide note, the anguish etched on his face just before he pulled the trigger, my confrontation with the reporter at the funeral home. Question were begging for answers. I didn't think this case was close to being over.

She interrupted my pregnant thoughts. "I don't understand you, Sidney. I thought this is what you live for."

No. What I lived for died nine months ago.

She leaned closer, her voice almost a whisper. "I know about your wife's death."

My head started spinning. How could she know? Molly's obituary hadn't mentioned those details. I'd made sure of that. And then it hit me.

Damn you, Eddie Baker.

I strode to the picture window with its panoramic view of the inlet. Specks of yellow in a sea of green leaves hinted at the arrival of fall. Cook Inlet sparkled. Somewhere out there I imagined a thirty-foot sloop, yours truly at the helm wearing a blue sweatshirt with the words **The Captain is Always Right** splashed across the front, Molly emerging from the cabin below, her honey-blonde hair flapping like a flag in the breeze.

God, I miss her.

My hand was shaking when I pulled the suicide note from my pocket, the image of Harvey sticking that gun in his mouth and the halo of blood that followed still very fresh in my mind. Somewhere in the distance, I heard a woman's voice. I gripped the note tightly enough to make the shaking stop.

Elizabeth was speaking. "I'm sorry, Sidney. I had no right—"

I cut her off. "I meant to give you this at the funeral." I handed her the piece of white paper. "I found it that night in the Tundra."

She unfolded it with a mixture of wonder and dread, then read it in silence while I read the unfolding sadness in her eyes. Afterward, she plucked a tissue from a burgundy dispenser and dabbed at her blue eyes. She sniffled and said, more to herself than to me, "My poor Harvey." Then, ever the stalwart soldier, she regained her composure and looked at me. "What do you make of this?"

"I think he was wracked with guilt over something. He couldn't deal with it."

"Deal with what?"

"I have no idea. One thing's for sure. He wanted you to leave Alaska."

She kept shaking her head. "But why?"

I shrugged. "He must have had a reason."

"Well, I'm not going anywhere until I know why he did this."

I turned to face the inlet and bit my lip. The woman's mind was made up. I knew there would be no dissuading her. I thought about all that had happened these last few days, how quickly everything had changed. When I turned back around she was staring at me, waiting for an answer.

Why did I have to open that damn door?

I sighed. "All right, Elizabeth, I'll do it. But I won't make you any promises. Are we clear about that?"

She nodded. "Just do your best. That's all I ask."

"I'll need to talk to friends, employees, anyone who knew him well. They'll be reluctant to speak candidly so I'll need you to contact them, let them know you expect their full cooperation."

"Consider it done."

I sat back down on the sofa and picked up my beer. "You know, this could end up being a waste of time."

"Fair enough." She picked up her wine glass. "I'll make a list of names and their contact information. What else do you need from me?"

"A few answers." I held up my empty bottle. "And another beer."

Soon I was holding my notebook, pen, and another Amber. The cold beer tasted good. I waited as Elizabeth replenished her wine glass and took a sip.

I flipped open my notebook. "Tell me about Harvey's friends."

She went to a built-in bookcase by the fireplace and returned with a brown leather photo album. She opened it and handed me a photo of three men sitting cross-legged around a campfire, each cradling a high-powered rifle in his arms. Two were immediately familiar: Joe Meacham, looking every bit the outdoorsman, and Harvey on the right. The third man—sitting in the middle behind the fire—was handsome, with a full head of dark hair and a cocky grin that reminded me of the jocks at my high school back in Ohio. The three men appeared at ease with each other—friends—but it was the fellow in the middle, with his air of supreme confidence, his features chiseled with character, who dominated the group.

Elizabeth leaned toward me and motioned with her index finger. "These two I think you know. That's Tom in the middle."

I commented that they must have been great friends.

"They were inseparable. Had been since childhood."

"When did you all meet?"

"Let's see. I transferred to McKinley High as a sophomore. We were in some of the same classes so I knew them casually that way. Tom and I started going steady our junior year. We were wed the summer after graduation." She stopped to sip wine. "We made a good life together." Her eyes sparkled in remembrance. "He began a successful career as a general contractor and I did quite well for myself in real estate."

"The three of them remained close after you two married?"

"Oh yes. They hunted, fished, played golf, you name it."

I gulped some beer. "Was it tough having to share him?"

She smiled. "Eddie Baker was right. You're good." She gripped the stem of her glass tightly. "I never resented Tom spending time with his buddies. It was what he loved to do. He gave me all the love and attention I needed. Who was I to deprive him of the things he loved?"

I marveled again at her strength of character. It was something that would no doubt remain with her long after her physical beauty had faded. Tom had seen it, too. He must have loved her deeply. I flipped through my notebook. "What else can you tell me about Joe?"

"After graduating, he earned his pilot's license and started a guide business with Bud Branigan. He eventually earned his master guide license. He and the boys went on hunting trips together every year without fail until . . ."

I stopped scribbling and glanced up. I could see the memory rushing back at her like a bore tide barreling through Turnagain Arm. "We don't have to do this now."

"No, it's all right." She inhaled a deep breath of air. "Tom had wanted to go to Kodiak Island to hunt brown bear that year, but Joe insisted on a moose hunt. He wanted a trophy for his den and had a spot picked out, so they packed up Joe's plane and headed out."

She reached for her glass, taking a tiny sip before setting it down again. "You know the rest of that story."

I waited while she composed herself. It didn't take long.

"Well, as you might imagine, it was a struggle after Tom died. The roughest year of my life. Thank God Harvey was there for me. I don't think I could have survived it without him. Joe was there for me too, but Harvey had a gentle side that, well, touched my heart. Somewhere along the way, we became more than friends." She paused, blushing. "It was no secret that he'd always had a crush on me."

I'll bet Harvey wasn't the only one.

"About three months ago I asked him to move in with me. I know that seems a little backward, but I wasn't too keen on squeezing into Harvey's one-bedroom condo." She gazed around the room. "And I couldn't imagine leaving this place." She glanced at me as if expecting a reaction. Seeing none, she continued. "With forty rapidly approaching, I did not intend to spend my remaining years alone. Harvey was a good and decent man. When I asked him to move in, he didn't hesitate."

"What about Joe? How does he fit in?"

Her mouth curled into a slight grin. "Joe has never hidden his feelings for me. We dated briefly in high school. Nothing serious."

"What happened?"

"That's a good question. He was tall and ruggedly handsome, a football star. All the girls were crazy about him."

"And you?"

She smiled faintly. "I found him a little too, for lack of a better word, possessive. I'm probably too independent for him. I must say, though, he's really been there for me since Harvey's death."

I nodded. My own first impression of Joe had not been a good one, but then first impressions are not always the best. I shifted the conversation. "What happens to Harvey's company now that he's passed?"

"In accordance with Harvey's will, all of his assets pass to me. It has to go through probate, of course."

"There are no next of kin?"

She shook her head. "None, I'm afraid. His parents are gone. He had an older brother who was killed in Vietnam. His marriage to Gloria bore no children."

"Who's running Aurora Electronics Supply now?"

She looked like she'd just swallowed a lemon. "Harvey's general manager, Paula Abernathy. That will change once I'm able to find a suitable replacement."

I scribbled the name in my notebook. "You don't like her?"

"She did everything she could to try to manipulate Harvey into giving her part interest in the company. And pardon me for saying so, but the woman's a tramp."

Gee, Elizabeth, tell me what you really think.

I leafed through my notes. "What more can you tell me about Bud Branigan?"

She looked thoughtful. "He and Joe were friends in high school. If I recall correctly, Bud had a background in business or accounting, which is why they partnered up. They're no longer in business together though. There was a parting of the ways some years back. I'm afraid that's all I can tell you."

I closed my notebook. "That will do for now. I can always call you if I think of anything else." I downed the last of my beer and Elizabeth walked me to the front door. She pulled Harvey's suicide note out of her shirt pocket and read it once more in silence before handing it back to me. "You should probably keep this, at least for now."

I stuffed the note in my shirt.

She shook her head slowly. "I wish he had confided in me more, but he was the silent type. He kept his feelings locked inside."

There's a lot of that going around.

"I still can't wrap my mind around this, Sidney. What on

earth would make him do something so extreme? That's what I need you to find out."

People react in different ways to highly emotional situations. Some cry. Some get angry. Elizabeth wanted answers. The trouble is, you don't always get the answers you want. Trying my best to sound reassuring, I said. "I'll do what I can. Somebody's bound to know something."

She smiled thinly. "I have faith in you, Sidney."

Moments later I slid behind the wheel of the Subaru. Thick gray clouds had begun to envelop the Hillside. As I thought about my new assignment, an ill-defined chill gripped me. I was about to follow Harvey Kahill down a rabbit hole. Where would it lead?

Nine

Half an hour later I sat on my sofa, case notes spread across the coffee table, wondering how on earth I let myself get dragged into this. Ah, yes. The money. Well, mostly the money.

I smiled knowing Elizabeth's generous retainer would have elicited a snarky comment from Molly. She detested the long, uncertain hours and the strain the all-night surveillances and late-night interviews had heaped on our marriage.

Priscilla scampered over to me. I scooped her up and scratched the underside of her chin, which sent her purring into overdrive. "How am I supposed to get any work done with you purring so loud I can't even hear myself think?" I returned her to solid ground and she shot me a look of annoyance.

I went into the kitchen, slapped a hamburger patty on the skillet, and smothered it in onions. Molly loved it when I cooked for her. We'd pretend we were in a fancy restaurant, feasting on steak or pasta dishes, Sinatra crooning in the background.

I returned to the couch and rested my plate on the coffee table, the Kahill file serving as a makeshift tablecloth. I bit into my burger and let my eyes drift over the sea of paper. Soon enough they landed on the suicide note, triggering a flashback to McHugh Creek. I pinched my eyes shut. When I opened them again I turned my gaze to the bookcase and the framed photograph of Molly looking radiant in a field of fireweed. My thoughts drifted back to the day I bought her the Smith and Wesson Ladysmith revolver for protection. Her reaction was classic Molly: "Why did you waste your money on such a thing? You know how I feel about guns."

Despite my insistence, she refused to take it, so I stuck it in a dresser drawer under a sweater and forgot about it.

Don't go there. Focus on the job at hand.

I bit off more burger and glanced at some notes I had scrawled concerning Joe Meacham. The sole surviving member of the Three Amigos was an obvious starting point. Perhaps the big man had some idea why Harvey would use his head for target practice. I made a plan to swing by his house in the morning after a trip to the courthouse.

After dinner, I crashed on the couch with a bottle of Corona. I twisted off the cap and sipped the cool liquid. Priscilla joined me, settling into my lap with two counterclockwise rotations. I admired her need to do that, even if I couldn't fathom the reason why. Maybe she didn't have a reason. That's the trouble with us humans. We have to have a reason for everything. Maybe cats circle before lying down for no other reason than they feel like it, and maybe people kill themselves for the same reason. Or not.

Elizabeth's need to know why Harvey killed himself echoed my own disjointed thoughts. Molly's death had never made any sense to me. She'd been depressed at times, but nothing serious. Or so I thought. I'd read that Alaska's high suicide rate was due to Seasonal Affective Disorder, or S.A.D., an unfortunate consequence of the long, dark winters, but I told myself such things only happened to other people, not to Molly.

I downed the contents of the clear bottle and sprawled out on the couch. Priscilla waited until I was settled in before adjusting herself to my new position. I tossed and turned long into the night, the stark images of the last few days flittering around in my head like so many bats in a deep, dark cave.

I woke just as filmy gray light began to fill my apartment, thankful for having been spared the nightmares. After showering, I smeared a dollop of strawberry preserves on an English muffin and wolfed it down. I was about to head out the door when I stopped short. If this was to be the return of Sidney Reed, Private Investigator, I needed to act the part. Returning to the bedroom, I opened the bottom drawer of my nightstand and pulled out a small black wallet-style leather case. I flipped it open to find a gold shield that bore the Alaska state seal and the words PRIVATE INVESTIGATOR embossed above and below it. I stuffed the case into my shirt pocket.

I threw open the door and was pelted with cold rain driven by a stiff north wind. Bracing myself, I trudged the two blocks to the Nesbett Courthouse, the newer of Anchorage's two courthouses, breezed through security, and was soon sitting at a computer terminal in the clerk's office.

What court research lacks in glamour and excitement, it makes up for in results—from tiny acorns grow mighty oaks, as the saying goes. In my years working as a P.I., rarely have court files failed to yield at least one nugget of useful information.

I typed Tom Landers' name into the search field and in a matter of seconds, the screen displayed a list of three cases. The most recent was a probate case. I wrote down the case number for later reference. The other two listings, both more than a decade old, were lawsuits in which Tom was listed as the plaintiff. Not surprising, considering he'd worked as a contractor. Those could also wait.

Next came Harvey. I found a "dissolution of marriage" from twelve years ago which I already knew about, but wrote down the number just in case. The remaining cases were traffic violations from years ago. Time to move on.

I keyed "Aurora Electronics Supply" into the search box and was rewarded with five case numbers. Four concerned small claims actions in which Aurora was the plaintiff. Probably petty theft or shoplifting. I pulled up the fifth case and things got a little more interesting—Aurora had been on the receiving end of a lawsuit filed two years ago. I noted with interest that Paula Abernathy, Aurora's general manager, was named as a co-defendant. I tore a blank off a pad next to the computer and filled in the relevant information before setting it aside. A separate search for Paula Abernathy produced no additional results.

The last name I checked—Joseph Meacham—yielded two hits, the first a "minor consuming" charge filed when Joe was seventeen. The second was a bit more interesting. Two years ago, a woman named Janet Foster had filed a domestic violence charge against him. The case had been dismissed, but Joe must have had a relationship with her. She definitely had interview potential, although I considered her a low priority at this point. In any event, in order to see the details of that case I'd have to walk next door to the Boney Courthouse where domestic files were housed.

I copied the screen details and stepped up to the service window. In the office space beyond, clerks went about their business. I was about to press the "Ring for Service" button when I spied a chunky, round-faced African American man in his mid-thirties heading in my direction.

"Sid!" He reached for my hand and shook it vigorously. "Long time, no see."

Court research would be a barely tolerable chore were it not for Martin "Marty" Johnson. Gregarious and upbeat, he never failed to lift my spirits and update me on the latest courthouse gossip.

"How've you been, Marty?"

He shrugged. "Same shit, different day. But it's great to see you, man!" Piercing brown eyes studied me carefully. "When I heard what happened to your wife, I couldn't believe it. I'm sorry, man."

I nodded.

"When you stopped coming in," he continued, "I figured you left the state."

"Why leave when I can be just as miserable here?"

He exhaled a belly laugh. "Good old Sid." His smile faded. "Dad left us when we were kids. Lost my momma to cancer at sixteen, so I know something about loss."

I started to speak, but he cut me off. "What I'm sayin' is, laughter's good an' all, but it only gets you so far. Don't try to go it alone."

"Thanks, Marty. You've always been good to me."

We shook hands and I handed him the form. "Can you pull a file for me?"

"Sure. As long as a judge ain't sittin' on it." He tapped his fingers on a keyboard and stared at a small computer terminal. "Got it. Be right back." He lumbered down a long hallway, returning moments later with a manila folder that he passed under a bar code reader and handed to me. "You know the drill," he said with a big-toothed grin.

I took the file. "Thanks, Marty. I won't forget what you said."

"You'll be all right, buddy," he said. "Life goes on."

I stepped into the viewing area—an expansive room with tables, chairs, several microfilm readers, and two copy machines. I took a seat at the nearest table and started with the folder captioned *Dennis Gandy v. Aurora Electronics Supply.* I flipped through the pages until I found the complaint, which I knew would give me the gist of what the lawsuit was about. In it, Gandy alleged that his boss, Paula Abernathy, had sexually harassed him over a period of several months, creating a hostile work environment that the company had allowed to occur.

Gandy provided three specific examples. On one occasion, Abernathy "touched his arm suggestively." On another, she referred to him as a "virile young man." In the third cited instance, Abernathy suggested that Gandy could advance his career within the company if he slept with her. Pretty vague stuff, the kind a good defense attorney can tear to pieces pretty handily. Predictably, the case was dismissed and Gandy got squat out of it.

I scrawled a few notes before dropping the file in the return box. When I stepped from the courthouse it was still raining, though not as hard. I pulled the hood of my jacket over my head and walked briskly to the parking garage. As I nestled behind the wheel of the Subaru, I found myself smiling. The weather sucked, I lived alone in a crappy apartment, I'd just witnessed a suicide, and nightmares kept me awake most nights.

But, damn, I was working again.

Ten

J oe Meacham lived in a weathered old log home situated on a heavily wooded parcel several acres in size with a clearing in the middle. The home consisted of a central structure and rooms that radiated out like spokes. I guessed it had begun life as a small cabin, with more rooms added over time, though not necessarily in adherence to sound construction practices. The various additions were connected unevenly and the roof sagged—an authentic Alaskan homestead.

I pulled into a gravel driveway pockmarked with ruts that were filled to the brim with rain from the downpour earlier. To my left, a felled tree sliced into two-foot lengths languished among the weeds like a dismembered sea monster. The sweet aroma of fresh-cut wood hung in the air.

When I opened the car door, my eardrums were assaulted by a crescendo of barking. From behind a screen door at the front of the house, a massive figure filled the doorframe. Behind him, two huge black-faced dogs barked themselves hoarse, trying in vain to muscle past their owner.

"Quiet!" Meacham barked back as I approached the doorway. He grabbed the two canines roughly by their studded collars and led them to somewhere inside the house. I heard a door slam and the barking trailed off. Moments later, heavy footfalls signaled his return. He pushed open the door wearing a red plaid shirt and blue jeans. If a theater had been casting for Paul Bunyan, he'd have gotten the part. Gray eyes bore into me.

"I'm Sidney Reed," I said. "We met yesterday at the funeral."

"Ah, yes, the detective. Liz told me you'd be stopping by. Well, don't just stand there, come on in."

He didn't offer a handshake, but I sensed it was not out of any disdain for me but rather a dislike of the formality of it. He certainly seemed pleasant enough now. A funeral home is probably not the best place to make character judgments.

I stepped inside a small mudroom—a uniquely Alaskan appendage that provides a welcome buffer between the cold exterior and the living area of the house. An assortment of coats, jackets, and headgear hugged both sides of the room, and all manner of footwear, from sneakers to hip waders and bunny boots, were lined up beneath them. Alaskan etiquette calls for the removal of footwear, but as I stooped to remove mine he let me know with a casual wave of his big hand that my shoes could remain on my feet.

"You're lucky to catch me at home. With hunting season almost here, I'm usually out at Lake Hood getting my plane and gear squared away."

"How's the season shaping up?"

He shrugged a pair of massive shoulders. "Can't complain. I'm all booked up for moose season. I also have a couple of fall bear hunts scheduled."

"Glad to hear it. I know how busy you must be. I'll try not to take up too much of your time."

"No trouble. Care for a beer?"

"You bet."

Meacham led me through the door at the opposite end of the mudroom and into a hallway. He motioned toward a room off to my left. "Have a seat in the den. I'll be right back."

Joe trudged off and I drifted into the room, letting my eyes adjust to the dim light from two small windows. His den could more accurately be called a trophy room. Stuffed and mounted animals were everywhere. There were ptarmigan, king salmon, wolf, deer, black and brown bear, lynx, and bison. The furnishings were sparse: sofa, table, a few chairs. Rifles of various makes and calibers rested on wall hooks or simply leaned against the wall in various parts of the room. A musty odor of undetermined origin hung in the air and I detected a hint of gun oil. A stone fireplace at one end lent the room the look and feel of a hunting lodge.

But it was the head of a huge bull moose mounted on the wall above the fireplace that grabbed my attention. Fascinated, I stepped closer. The taxidermist had done his job well. Dark, sunken eyes radiated cold rage, and nostrils flared from the bull's long, angular snout. The spread of its antlers could not have been an inch less than six feet, with four spear-like tines on each side. I'd seen a lot of moose in my twenty years in Alaska, both alive and dead, but this one was, without doubt, the biggest I'd ever laid eyes on. It was also, thankfully, dead.

"Impressive, isn't it?" Meacham's voice boomed behind me.

I spun around to find Meacham grinning and holding two bottles of Alaskan Amber.

"Excuse me if I startled you." He handed me one of the bottles.

I nodded and said, "Yes, very impressive." I sipped from the ice-cold bottle as the two of us stood looking at his trophy.

"That's him, you know." He stared at the moose.

His meaning failed to register. I said, "Him who?"

"The moose that killed Tom."

I thought back to what Elizabeth had told me about that fateful hunting trip. How they were stalking a large bull moose and Joe had shot it, though not before it charged Tom, killing him. Joe had mounted the head of that moose on his wall as a souvenir. I let that sink in.

I finally managed to say, "Got to be some kind of record."

"Made the Boone & Crockett record book." He said it with unconcealed pride.

Boone & Crockett is the big game hunter's equivalent of the Academy Awards. I congratulated him, but in truth I wanted very badly to pin his hide to the wall next to the moose. I'd hunted a fair amount in my life, but thanks largely to Molly's influence I'd come to dislike trophy hunting. Common sense told me the pursuit of trophies robs the gene pool of the best breeding stock. And anyway, my interactions with trophy hunters had led me to conclude that, for many of them, it was more about vanity than anything else.

"Do you hunt, Reed?" he said, interrupting my musings on human taxidermy and the male ego.

"Some. I hunted whitetail and pheasant as a boy. I've hunted small game up here, but that's about it. Never seem to find the time."

He answered with a grunt.

I looked up at him. "If you don't mind me asking, what happened out there?"

He measured his words. "Harvey, Tom, and I have hunted together for years. That year we flew to a small lake about eighty miles upriver from Dillingham and set up a base camp. I knew there were some big bulls in that country. The first couple of days we saw a few females and lots of sign, but no bulls. Near the end of the third day, I spotted a big one working his way through a river drainage, so we made a plan to stalk him. I calculated his likely path and we set up in a line about eighty yards long, with Tom in the middle. We all agreed he had the first shot if it worked out that way. Well, we waited and, sure enough, we hear him coming—snorting and blustering up a storm. A rutting bull can be pretty ornery."

I had found the same to be true of the moose's smaller cousin, the whitetail deer, when I'd hunted them as a boy. The males can get pretty crazy during the mating season. I'd heard stories of hunters being gored by a hotheaded buck.

Joe chugged some Amber and wiped his mouth with the back of his hand. "Anyway, from where I stood I saw the bull headed for Tom, and it dawned on me Tom couldn't see him. I know this 'cause the bull's only forty, fifty feet away and Tom still hadn't leveled his rifle. Well, that got me a little worried so I put my scope on him and saw the hairs standing up on the back of his neck. He was pawing the ground, too. I realized he was about to charge so I took my rifle off safety and right then the bull lowered his head and charged right at Tom, goin' like a locomotive."

Meacham paused for another sip of beer and looked to make sure he had my full attention, enjoying the role of storyteller.

"I knew I only had one chance at a kill. He was charging through an alder thicket so my view was limited, but I kept the crosshairs where I thought his shoulder was and squeezed. As soon as I got off a shot I ran flat out to where Tom was. Well, there was a furious commotion up there, like all hell had broke loose. I heard Tom scream and Harvey call out from the other side of him. When I got there Tom was on the ground, messed up pretty bad, the bull lying next to him. I'd hit him, all right—fatally—but he still had enough juice left in him to do in poor Tom. It's the adrenalin, you know. I'm gonna grab another beer. You want one?"

I glanced at my half-full bottle and waved him off. "I'm good."

I watched him walk out of the room and shook my head. He'd just described the death of his friend as calmly as a clerk pours over the day's receipts. This guy was a cool customer. I stared up at that massive head on the wall, trying to imagine what was running through Tom's mind during those last few seconds of his life. Joe came through the door, interrupting my thoughts.

"Ironically," he continued, as though he'd never left, "it turned out to be a world record bull, or, more accurately, *the* world record bull."

This is world record bull, all right.

"What did you use to bring this big boy down, an elephant gun?"

"You could say that." He reached for a rifle leaning against the wall to his left. "Remington Model 700, chambered for

.375 H&H Magnum." He strummed his fingers along the stock slowly, almost caressingly. "I use it for all my big game hunting." Handing it to me, he said, "The perfect rifle for large game. Packs a big wallop, though too late to save my friend, I'm afraid."

I pulled the bolt back to clear the weapon. A round summersaulted out of the chamber and clattered on the floor.

"I keep it loaded, of course," he said with a grin.

"Of course." I hefted the gun, noting it was clean and well oiled. Joe took good care of his firearms. I handed him the rifle. He bent down and picked the round up off the floor and re-chambered it before returning the gun to its home against the wall.

I said, "Mind if I ask you a few questions?"

"Knock yourself out." Joe motioned toward a hunter green sofa as he eased his massive frame into a matching chair. He poured beer into his mouth, gulping down nearly half the bottle in one go.

"Thanks for seeing me." I took out my notebook. "Elizabeth has asked me to inquire into Harvey's suicide."

"Goddamn waste of time if you ask me." With one more tip of his bottle he finished off beer number two. I downed the rest of mine and he grabbed it without comment. "I'll get us another."

As I waited I felt uneasy. Something about this guy bothered me. For one thing, it was the day after Harvey's funeral and he hadn't expressed a word of remorse for his best friend. Then there was the way he bragged about killing the moose. It seemed odd to me.

Joe returned and handed me one of two beers and sat down. "Okay, Reed, fire away."

I sipped some beer and said casually, "How long had you known Harvey?"

He exhaled a long sigh. "Since high school. We were in the same class at McKinley. Couple of football jocks who became friends and stayed that way for twenty years."

"What was he like?"

"He was generous. If I needed something, all I had to do was ask. He loved the outdoors. Hunting, fishing, you name it. We went all over the state, the three of us."

"Three?"

"Me, Harv, and Tom Landers."

I drank some more Amber. "In your airplane?"

He looked at me like I was from another planet. "You have to fly if you want to get anywhere in this state. When the other guys were asking their parents for cars, I was saving up to buy an airplane. You can drive two hours up to Montana Creek and launch a raft if you want to, but I'd rather spend an afternoon on Lake Iliamna any day. That's just me."

"Was anything bothering him?"

He took a long swig of beer. "Not that I know of. He seemed like a pretty happy guy."

"Were he and Elizabeth having any problems?"

He shot me a look. "No. There were no problems."

"How did those two meet?"

"Through Tom, I think. He and Liz dated pretty steady all through high school before getting hitched. Harv met Gloria in college and they got married, but that didn't last."

"What happened?"

Joe shrugged. "He told me they weren't soul mates, whatever that means. He finally divorced her. After Tom died, he and Liz started seeing more of each other."

"Are you sure there were no problems between them?"

He stared at me with steely gray eyes. "What's this really about, Reed?"

"I'm trying to find out why he killed himself."

Joe finished a long pull on his Amber before speaking. "You understand, I don't want to see Liz hurt by dragging this out longer than necessary. So in the interest of seeing this investigation of yours end as soon as possible, I'll be frank with you."

I nodded. I like it when people are frank with me.

He leaned forward in his chair, making sure he had my attention. "Harvey had something going on with the gal running his company."

"Paula Abernathy?" I recalled what my client had said about Harvey's business manager. "What makes you say that?"

Meacham threw me a knowing glance. "When you're as close as Harv and I were, you don't have secrets."

I thanked him for his candor.

"Don't mention it. If you're any good at what you do, an interview with her will confirm what I'm telling you. Then maybe you can wrap this up and give Liz some peace."

"You think Harvey killed himself over an affair?"

"What else could it be?"

I was skeptical of that theory, but Paula was next on my interview list. Maybe she could shed light on that one. I said, "Thanks, I'll check it out" and scribbled a note. "I understand Harvey took Tom's death especially hard. Is it possible the strain was too much for him?"

His fist tightened almost imperceptibly around the bottle of Amber. "That's nonsense. Tom was my best friend and his death was a great loss, but I'm not about to blow my brains out over it."

I pondered his response as I poured some Amber down my throat. "Maybe he felt guilty for not being able to save Tom's life?" My own guilt rumbled to the surface as my thoughts flashed to Molly.

"You're way off base, Reed. No way was that his fault."

Something about his reaction to my questions was gnawing at me. I said, "Was there any sort of trouble between you and Tom?"

He frowned. "I thought you were investigating Harvey? What does Tom have to do with it?"

"Well, the three of you were close friends. What was it the Three Musketeers used to say? One for all and all for one?"

"Look, I've told you everything I know. I don't know why Harvey killed himself, unless it had something to do with that Abernathy woman. I doubt if anyone else knows, except maybe Harvey. Why don't you ask him?"

I would if that .357 slug hadn't ground his brain into hamburger.

I decided on a different tack. "Is it possible Elizabeth was cheating on Harvey?"

Meacham catapulted out of his seat like he was strapped to a Saturn Five rocket. "Fuck you, Reed! Liz would never have cheated on Harvey. Or Tom. Never!" He hovered over me, his posture menacing. He was just getting warmed up. "Liz is a great gal and I'll be damned if I'm going to let you talk about her like this. As for Harvey, I don't have a clue as to why he killed himself. He had something going on with that slut at Aurora, so maybe that was it. Tom's death certainly hit him hard. Maybe he couldn't deal with it, I don't know. But Liz, a cheater? That dog won't hunt."

The veins in his bull neck twitched like night crawlers in a bait bucket. I decided this guy had a serious anger management problem, not to mention strong feelings for Elizabeth. But was there something else?

I let another sip of Amber pass between my lips and looked at him. "When someone commits suicide, there's always a reason. I intend to find out why."

He slowly sat back down. "Pardon my anger. It's just that Liz is very special to me and she's vulnerable right now. Bad enough her losing Tom, but now with Harvey's suicide . . . It's tearing her apart."

I switched gears. "When did you last see Harvey?"

"Couple of weekends ago. We flew out to Skilak Lake for some fishing."

"Did he seem upset then?"

"No more than usual."

"Usual? I thought you said he was a happy guy?"

His neck muscles twitched again. "He . . . he never got over Tom's death."

"That was two years ago. Could it have been something else?"

"I don't know what that would be."

"You two were friends, weren't you?"

"Of course we were. I told you that."

"He never came to you and said, Joe, something's bothering me? Perhaps confided in you on Skilak Lake?"

"No, he didn't. I don't know what you're getting at, Reed, but this conversation is going nowhere. For the last time, I don't know why he killed himself and I'm sick and tired of answering your stupid fucking questions."

I didn't know why irritating him felt so good, but it did. "Just trying to get some closure for Elizabeth."

His eyes were fixed on mine. "If you really want to give her closure, leave us both the hell alone."

I studied the deepening lines in his forehead and the tiny micro-tremors in his jaw muscles. I'd definitely touched a nerve. I'd also reached the point of diminishing return. You have to know when to stop.

I stood up. "Okay, Joe. Thanks for the beer. I'll let myself out."

I moved to the door and glanced back. I half expected him to follow me, but he just sat there staring at the seat I'd just vacated. I looked up one last time at the massive moose head hanging on the wall before heading out the door.

Eleven

My interview with Joe Meacham was still on my mind on the drive to Midtown. I'd gone in with no expectations and came out with lots of questions, but they'd have to wait a while for answers. One thing was crystal clear though: Joe Meacham was hiding something. But what?

Aurora Electronics Supply was easy enough to find. The company's large storefront window was plastered with advertisements for two-way radios, security alarms, and other assorted electronic gear. I angle-parked in front of a large sign that read ALL CABLES 25% OFF! in bold black letters. I arrived half an hour before closing time after calling ahead for an appointment with Paula Abernathy, Aurora's general manager—the same Paula Abernathy my client intended to fire as soon as she got the chance and who, according to Joe Meacham, had been doing the wild thing with Harvey Kahill.

This should be interesting.

I stepped through the front door and paused to get the lay of the land. Behind the checkout area, rows of industrial shelving stocked with electronics gear ran the length of the store. A half dozen customers strolled the aisles. There were three cash registers, all manned by young men in their late teens and early twenties. I thought about the Dennis Gandy court file and wondered how many of these guys Paula Abernathy had hit on.

I strode up to a gangly kid whose face was pockmarked with acne. His nametag read **KENNY G.** "So the rumors are true," I said. "You gave up the saxophone for retail sales."

He looked at me like I was from Jupiter. "Ah, sorry sir, I don't play the saxophone."

"You are Kenny G, are you not?"

He looked at his nametag, then at me. "Yes, but I don't play any instruments. You must have me confused with someone else."

I gave up on the Kenny G bit. Wrong generation, I guess. "I'm here to see Ms. Abernathy. She's expecting me."

He pointed between two aisles toward the rear of the store. "Through those double doors, first door on the left."

I pushed past the doors and entered a dimly lit hallway that had two faded brown doors facing each other. The one on the left held a sign that read **PAULA**, the one opposite, **HARVEY**. I twisted the knob on Harvey's door—locked. I turned and knocked on Paula's door and a sultry voice said, "Come in."

I entered a small, brightly lit office, in the center of which stood a plain-looking gray metal desk. Behind it stood a tall, attractive woman who was anything but plain. She came around the desk and said, "Mr. Reed, I presume. I'm Paula Abernathy."

She wore a powder blue dress that stopped at mid-thigh. Chestnut hair flowed off her shoulders and down her back in silky waves. Her copper skin told me she was either hitting the tanning bed twice a week or making regular trips to Maui. Her legs looked good enough to distract the average breathing male—a category that, despite my recent trials and tribulations, included me. She looked to be in her late thirties and showed no sign of losing her ability to turn heads, and yet there was a trampiness about her that put me off. I pictured Molly's natural beauty and my heart ached.

We shook hands. I said, "Please, call me Sidney."

I flashed my badge. I didn't think I needed to, but I wanted to see how impressed she'd be. She studied it intently, then looked at me, long black eyelashes fluttering. Definitely impressed.

"Please, call me Paula." She gestured toward a faded yellow armchair and glided toward an identical chair opposite mine. A sharp click drew my gaze to her black three-inch heels. With a rustling of fabric, she settled into the depths of the chair, the movement hiking the hemline of her dress noticeably. A good detective misses nothing.

She crossed her legs in slow motion and smiled as if to say, *Aren't I something?* She was something, all right.

"How may I help you, Sidney?"

"Well, Paula, as I explained to you on the phone, Elizabeth Landers hired me."

"Yes, she called me. Of course, I'll cooperate fully." She batted those lashes again. "What would you like to know?"

I pulled out my notebook. "Tell me about Harvey."

Her eyes welled up with tears, and not the crocodile variety. She really did miss the guy. I shuffled the few steps to the desk and snatched up the box of tissue that lay there. I held it out as an offering and she plucked one out.

"I'm sorry," she said, dabbing her eyes. "We're all in shock over this."

"Take your time." I returned to my chair and waited while she composed herself.

After a moment she stopped dabbing. "What can I say? He was a wonderful man. He treated his employees very well, but he also had a good head for business. Started with nothing and built the company from the ground up."

"Have you been with the company long?"

"Practically from the beginning." She paused to dab some more. "I met Harvey at UAA, where I was completing my business degree. He had a good eye for talent."

"I can see that."

She smiled, her teeth gleaming like high beams.

"I gather he'd been married once."

She folded her hands around her knee. "Yes. He and Gloria married young. Too young, as it turned out. The marriage lasted eight years, but it was over way before that if you know what I mean."

I'd seen too many marriages end that way to disagree.

"Can you think of a reason why Harvey would want to take his own life?"

She shook her head sadly. "I've been asking myself that question since it happened. Harvey was always a happy guy, and he loved this business. It makes no sense."

"How was Aurora doing financially?"

"Quite well. It was tough in the early years, but Harvey worked his butt off to make a go of it. We've turned a profit now for nine consecutive years."

"Notice any change in his behavior in the last few weeks or months?"

She fidgeted with the tissue. "Harvey wasn't himself for a long time after Tom's death."

"Tom Landers?"

She nodded. "It wasn't until his relationship with Elizabeth blossomed that I began to see a change in him. Once those two got together, he was on top of the world, until—." She paused.

I leaned forward. "Until what?"

She sighed. "A couple of weeks ago he and his friend Joe Meacham flew out to one of the lakes on the Kenai for some fishing. I think it was Skilak. When he came back he started acting . . . well, strange."

"Strange how?"

"Pacing around, acting nervous, distraught." She hesitated, her brow arching in concern. "It doesn't make sense, but . . ."

"Yes?"

"He acted like . . . like he was afraid of something."

"Afraid of what?"

"I don't know. I tried to get him to tell me, but he said I shouldn't worry about it."

I looked at her. "Anything else?"

"I'm sorry, no."

I scribbled in my notebook and then looked at her. "Tell me more about Tom."

"I didn't see him much. Every so often I'd be at Harvey's place for a get-together and Tom would be there. He came into the store from time to time. Harvey spoke of him quite a bit."

"Tell me about their relationship."

"They were close, I know that. Never heard Harv say a bad word about him, ever. He looked up to Tom. He was devastated when Tom was killed."

"He must have been quite a guy."

She rubbed a strand of hair idly between her thumb and forefinger. "I would say Tom was everything Harvey wanted to be: movie-star handsome, charming, adventurous. Don't get me wrong, Harvey was no slouch in the charm department, but Tom was a real jock, a man's man. An over-achiever, you might say."

"What about Elizabeth?"

Her eyes flitted about, searching for the right words. "She's smart. Classy. The boys knew Liz from McKinley High, where I gather she was quite popular. Prom queen, valedictorian, you name it."

"And sought after by every guy in school, I imagine."

"She turned heads for sure, but it was kismet between her and Tom pretty much from the beginning. The other guys never had a chance."

I detected a twinge of jealousy but left it alone. "How did Harvey feel about their relationship?"

She chuckled. "Little did she know when she married Tom that Harvey and Joe would be part of the package, too. I remember her joking that at times she felt like she was married to three men instead of one."

"Was Harvey jealous of Tom?"

"Not at all," she shot back. "He was happy for him."

I thought about the third Amigo. "What about Joe?"

She looked thoughtful. "I always felt—and this is just my opinion—that Joe was never quite in the same league with the other two. He always seemed to follow Tom and Harv around because he wanted to be close to Elizabeth. He obviously had the hots for her." She lowered her voice, as though worried someone would overhear us. "I heard he and Tom got into it a couple of times."

"Did they ever come to blows?"

She stretched out her fingers, inspecting her flame-red nails thoughtfully. "So I hear. You'll have to ask Elizabeth about that."

You bet your strappy heels I will.

I made a show of studying my notes, then looked up and fixed her with a gaze. "Were you and Harvey having an affair?"

Her eyes widened and drifted up and to the right. Eyes are amazing things. They're not only windows to the soul, but also remarkably good lie detectors. I understood neurolinguistics enough to know she was constructing a new memory.

She touched her fingers to her chest. "Harvey and me having an affair? That's just—"

"Paula, stop," I said, raising a hand. "I know about the affair, okay?"

She feigned shock. Shock morphed into a blush.

"Okay, look, I'll level with you. When Gloria left him, he was a lonely man. Ours was a close relationship, working nights a lot to make the business successful. There was an attraction between us. One thing led to—"

"When did it end?" I said impatiently.

She stared at her folded palms. "Sometime in the spring. One evening he told me we couldn't do it anymore, that he and Elizabeth had started up a relationship."

"Did she know about you two?"

"I don't think he told her." She gave me a questioning look. "You wouldn't . . ."

"No, I wouldn't."

She visibly relaxed. "Thank you, Sidney. He loved her very much. It would hurt her if she knew."

"Okay." I was pretty sure she was more worried it would

hurt *her* if Elizabeth knew. For my part, I didn't see any point in telling her about it. I figured she probably knew. There wasn't much that escaped her keen eyes.

I flipped through my notebook until I found my jottings from the courthouse. "Tell me about Dennis Gandy."

She flinched almost imperceptibly. "Are you trying to shock me, Sidney?"

I smiled back. "We P.I.'s are a crafty bunch."

"Indeed you are." Her eyes ranged over me. "And not bad looking either. But what does that young man's frivolous lawsuit have to do with poor Harvey's death?"

"I like to cover all the bases."

She leaned back, which had the effect of nudging her hemline slightly upward. "I have fond memories of Dennis. Nice kid, though a bit of a momma's boy. He apparently found my presence around the business a little, shall we say, distracting?" She uncrossed then re-crossed her legs and batted her eyes seductively for good measure. Subtlety was not her strong suit.

"Harvey and I ran the business like a family," she continued. "It may not have been as politically correct as some would wish, but everyone was happy. Well, almost everyone. Apparently, Dennis's mommy was in the store one day and saw me hugging her little boy and she flipped out. I guess she thought his duties here included getting raped in the stockroom or some such nonsense. She filed a sexual harassment suit against the company. The case was thrown out, of course."

"Of course." I closed my notebook. For all I knew, she'd screwed every guy who'd ever worked at Aurora, but aside from the titillation factor, my gut told me delving into Paula's sexual escapades would bring me no closer to finding out why Harvey decided to eat a bullet.

I rose from my chair. "Thanks for your time, Paula. You've been a big help."

"My pleasure, Sidney. I'll walk you to the door."

We strolled to the front of the store, where Kenny was dutifully sweeping the floor near the registers. Everyone else was gone. The fading light of evening streamed in through the storefront window.

"Will you lock up for the night, Kenny?"

"Yes, Ms. Abernathy."

Once we were outside, Paula turned to me. "Tell me, Sidney. Who is she?"

"Beg your pardon?"

"I know when I'm not being subtle. I've all but mailed you a personal invitation. There must be another woman in your life. If you don't mind my asking, who is she?"

I pictured Molly sitting contentedly in her rocking chair with a book, the cat curled up in her lap. "Priscilla," I said. "Her name is Priscilla."

"Well, she's a lucky woman. If you two don't work out, you know where to find me."

I conjured up a mental image of Priscilla gripping a ballpoint pen in her tiny little paw as she signed divorce papers. Knowing her, that cat would take me for everything I had—if I had anything worth taking.

Paula strolled over to a baby blue Nissan Sentra, her heels clicking sharply on the pavement. I climbed into the Subaru and watched her scoot behind the wheel, her dress nearly reaching the tops of her tanned thighs. She shut the door and smiled at me through the window before pulling into the street. Yeah, she was something, all right. I wasn't surprised to learn she and Harvey had had an affair. The woman tossed out pheromones like beads in a Mardi Gras parade.

I eased back into the seat, replaying the interview in my mind. I was inclined to believe her story that their affair had ended before he started dating Elizabeth. Still, I had to rule out all possibilities. Maybe there was a way to confirm her story about the affair.

I relaxed behind the wheel and waited for Kenny. Every so often his lanky form appeared behind the storefront window. When he was done sweeping he donned a light gray jacket and came outside swinging a chubby bundle of keys. He locked up and headed for an older black Ford pickup. I met him at the driver's door.

"Hi, Kenny."

He turned. "Oh, it's you again. I told you, man, I don't know that other Kenny dude."

I let him have a peek at my badge. The evening sun glinted off the shiny metal. His eyes widened.

"Hey, am I in some kinda trouble?"

"Relax. I just want to ask you about Harvey."

Visibly relieved, he said, "I guess it's okay to talk to you. Yeah, that was a real bummer, him killing himself like that. Mr. Kahill was a good guy."

"Ms. Abernathy must have taken it pretty hard."

"Yeah, she was crying and stuff."

I eyed him knowingly. "I heard they were very close, if you know what I mean." I winked for good measure.

He shrugged. "Sure, they were a thing for a while, but he ended it."

"When was that?"

Kenny glanced around as if fearing Paula might be watching him. "Is it okay for me to be telling you this stuff?"

I nodded reassuringly. "This is between us guys."

"Mr. Kahill broke it off about six months ago."

"How do you know?"

"I overheard him telling her it was over. That he was with Elizabeth now."

"Elizabeth?"

"Don't know her last name. Nice lookin' blonde 'bout Mr. Kahill's age. Stops by the store from time to time."

"How did you find out about the affair?"

Kenny grinned. "It was common knowledge around this place. No big deal, really. He was divorced. Paula, ah, Ms. Abernathy, well, you saw how she is. Let's face it, the woman's a—she gets around."

"What about her husband?"

"What about him? I'm sure he knew about it. She told me she has his permission to do whatever she wants."

My eyes drilled into him. "Even with the hired help?"

He looked at me fearfully. "It's not like that anymore, not since—"

"Since Dennis Gandy filed a lawsuit?"

"Yeah, that's right. Look, man, I can't afford to lose this job. It pays well, I get two weeks—"

"Relax, Kenny. I'm not interested in your love life. I'm just trying to figure out why Harvey blew his brains out."

He visibly relaxed. "You and everyone else. It was so frickin' weird. It's all everyone's been talking about since it happened."

"How did you find out?"

"On Saturday morning, Paula called all of us into her office and broke the news. Then she sent everyone home and closed for the day. She was pretty broken up over it."

"Why do you think he did it?"

He shook his head slowly. "Beats the hell out of me. He seemed pretty happy, but what do I know?"

"What about Aurora? Were there any problems?"

"Not that I know of. The business was doing well. Mr. K said so. He loved coming to work."

"Notice him acting differently the last couple of weeks?"

His eyes lit up. "Now that you mention it, he was kinda nervous and fidgety the last couple of weeks. Kept his door shut a lot. Never figured he'd off himself though." He looked at his wristwatch. "Dude, I gotta run. My girlfriend's waiting for me to pick her up."

"Thanks for the chat," I said.

He climbed into the Ford, revved the engine, and leaned out the open window. "Sure hope you figure this out."

Black soot puffed out of the Ford's tailpipe as Kenny pulled out into the street.

"Me, too," I said to no one.

Twelve

Twenty minutes later I twisted the cap off a Corona and settled into the couch. Priscilla soon joined me, nestling snugly into my lap. I thumbed the TV remote and landed on an immaculately groomed Anderson Cooper interviewing some dirtbag on CNN. I clicked it off and eased back into the couch. My mind strayed to the Kahill case.

Paula's affair with Harvey seemingly had ended when he became intimate with Elizabeth, effectively ruling out the guilt-over-an-affair theory. It also meant Joe Meacham had lied to me. Why smear the name of a close friend? Was he trying to steer me away from something else?

Joe and Harvey's fishing trip to Skilak Lake showed promise. Harvey began acting strangely right after that. Had something happened on that trip?

The common thread running through the case seemed to be Tom Landers' death, but something wasn't adding up. I could understand Harvey being distressed about the loss of his friend, but suicide? Tom died two years ago. Why kill himself now, three months before his wedding to Elizabeth? I decided to drive out to Elizabeth's place first thing in the morning and let her know what I'd been up to.

My eyelids grew heavy—the alcohol was doing its work. Halfway through my third beer, I noted Priscilla had given up trying to sit on my lap and relocated to the rocker. I turned the TV back on and, after a bit more channel surfing, landed on the Sci-Fi channel just in time to see a cute blonde gobbled up by what looked like a giant ostrich.

I woke just shy of 7 a.m., drenched in my own sweat. That

damn dream had returned with a vengeance, but with a new twist: This time Molly and Harvey faced off with semi-automatic weapons at ten paces in a bizarre duel.

How much more of this can I take?

I shook it off, dressed, and headed downstairs. Behind the counter, Rachel Saint George had her nose in a paperback book. An older couple at the rickety table by the window shared a bowl of soup. Next to them, a woman whose face was angled away from me—her dark brown locks cascading in waves over her shoulders like a waterfall—sipped coffee. I ambled up to the counter and cleared my throat. Rachel glanced up, feigning surprise.

"I must be seeing things. The Sidney Reed I know never gets up before 9 a.m."

When I didn't take the bait, she frowned. "Why the sad face? Somebody fill your cookie jar with moose nuggets?"

"Bad dream," I muttered.

Rachel smiled.

I bristled. "Reveling in the misfortunes of others, Ms. Saint George?"

"On the contrary, Mr. Reed. I have just the thing to cheer you up." She pointed to the girl with the cascading hair.

"Who is she?" I wanted to know.

"Didn't say. She seems eager to talk to you though." Grinning impishly, Rachel said, "Go get 'em, tiger."

"Not interested. Go play cupid with some other sap."

Rachel's smile left her. She leaned across the counter. "Pardon me if I get all motherly on you, but it's been almost a year now. Time to move on."

I shot her a withering look and strolled over to the mystery girl, who was sipping from a brown beverage cup, her head buried in a newspaper. A second cup rested on the table. I studied the quaffed mane of chestnut hair for a moment before it came to me.

I said, "Well, if it isn't God's gift to print journalism."

Maria Maldonado glanced up. "Good morning, Mr. Reed. I've been waiting for you."

"You aren't stalking me, are you, Ms. Maldonado?"

She smiled. It was a beautiful smile. "Would a stalker bring you coffee?" She gestured toward the second cup. "Rachel told me your preference."

"Did she now?"

"I assure you, Mr. Reed, I come in peace. Have a drink with me. Please."

I eased into the chair, stared at the cup in front of me, and mumbled, "Thank you."

I hadn't expected to see her again. I only knew that if I did, I'd give her a piece of my mind for the funeral home confrontation.

"Miss Maldonado, what are—"

"Please, call me Maria." Her voice had a soothing quality to it. I find the female voice attractive, although I've never understood why. Maybe it's the frequency or something.

"All right, Maria. What's this about?"

Her eyes were chocolate brown and round as coasters. She lowered them demurely. "I came to apologize."

I leaned back in my chair. "Oh?"

"For accosting you at the funeral."

"I see. And what was that nonsense about Harvey Kahill being murdered?"

She sipped daintily. "Two years ago, I covered a story about a man who was killed on a moose hunting trip in western Alaska."

"Let me guess. Tom Landers."

"That's a pretty good guess."

"I'm a pretty good guesser. Go on."

She fidgeted nervously with her cup. "I was new to the paper then. When my editor handed me the story, I wanted desperately to make a good impression. I spent a great deal of time on it; too much, apparently. He ordered me to stop or find another job."

"Then what happened?"

"They ran the story, but something wasn't right."

I sipped some mocha. "What do you mean?"

Maria leaned forward and I caught a hint of lavender. "A source at Fish and Game hinted that there was something fishy about the guy's death."

"Fishy how?"

"Something about the nature of the injuries."

"Who was your source?"

She looked away. "I can't divulge—"

"Can't divulge sources. I get it. What about the injuries?"

"He was pretty vague. When I pressed him for details, he clammed up. I had the feeling he was worried about getting in trouble with his boss." She paused to watch a short, bedraggled Native man stagger past the window in the direction of Third Street, a sad reminder of Anchorage's homeless problem. "After the story ran, I moved on to other things but kept that little gem in my back pocket thinking I could develop it into something later if the opportunity presented itself. Sure enough, something did."

"Harvey Kahill's suicide."

She nodded. "When I heard about it, my curiosity was piqued. First Landers and now Kahill. It seemed too coincidental."

"Must have been a real gotcha moment for you." I bit my tongue as soon as I said it.

Her lips puckered. "Please don't mock me, Mr. Reed." She glared at me before snatching up her cup and taking a sip.

"Sorry," I said. "Go on."

"I'd been working the courthouse beat for over year, which gave me some street cred with my editor. He gave me the green light to do a little digging. A law enforcement source of mine told you were at the scene, so I checked our clip files and found your photo and some news clippings. I must say, your career as a private investigator is quite impressive, Mr. Reed. Anyway, when I went to Kahill's funeral to see who might show up, I recognized you from your photo. Figured I'd try to get an interview."

"You thought Harvey might have been murdered? That's quite a leap from suicide."

"Quite a big leap, actually, but I had a hunch. And I thought if I could prove he was murdered, my future at the paper would be secure. Admittedly, ambition clouded my judgment. When I learned about Mr. Kahill's death, I thought his and Landers' death might be tied together, that you might be involved in some way. I don't think that now."

"What are you talking about? Involved how?"

"Well, my source said—"

"It's Pendleton, isn't it?" Anger welled up inside me like rancid bile.

Her perfect little nose scrunched up in disapproval. "You know a reporter can't reveal her sources."

"Pendleton's not a source. He's a mistake."

Someone must have fiddled with the volume control on my mouth when I wasn't looking. Heads turned in our direction. Maria stared. Rachel's voice boomed from behind the counter. "Easy, big fella."

I raised my hands like a priest dispensing a blessing and looked at Maria. "Pendleton and I have a history. Let's just leave it at that."

She shrugged. "Okay."

"Seriously, though, Pendleton was your source, right?"

She held up a palm. "No comment."

"Hey, that's my line!"

We both laughed and the tension between us melted away. As she downed the last of her drink, I studied her closely for the first time. She was about thirty, with a roundish face and full lips. Her eyes were wide and seemed to reflect light from all directions. The plaid shirt and black slacks from the funeral had been replaced with a knee-length paisley skirt, beige blouse, and black high-heeled boots. Her hair was shiny and bounced as if she'd washed and blow-dried it moments before. Her skin had a slight olive tint, suggesting Hispanic heritage.

I said, "Tell you what. I promise not to ask you the identity of your sources if you promise not to accost me at funerals."

That elicited the kind of smile poets pen lines about.

She said, "You've got a deal, Mr. Reed."

"One more thing. Call me Sidney."

"All right, Sidney."

I slouched in my chair, feeling strangely at ease for the first time in a long while. "What changed your mind about me?"

Maria looked down at her coffee cup, picking nervously at the plastic lid. "When I read about your wife's death, I was touched. I realized I had no right making such an accusation without proof. I should have known better. I wanted to make it right."

I studied her in silence. Her neck was long and graceful and when she spoke she had a habit of tilting her head to one side. There was something else, too: an eerie sadness in her voice and in her eyes.

"Sidney, are you listening? I'm trying to apologize here."

"You really want to make it right?"

"I do."

"Then let me buy you dinner."

Her mouth fell open. "You want to buy me dinner?"

"Yes."

She thought for a moment. "All right. I guess. I mean, sure."

"Good. How does this Saturday night sound?"

"Works for me."

"I'll pick you up at eight, then."

"I'll be ready."

She jotted her address on the back of a business card and handed it to me. "I have to get back to work. Got a deadline to meet." She rose from her chair. "I'd like to know more about the Kahill suicide. Off the record, of course."

I stood and we shook hands. Maintaining a reasonably good poker face, I said, "I'll see you on Saturday."

She smiled demurely. "Thank you, Sidney."

Moments later she was out the door.

Rachel came up next to me and said, "Pretty lady." She laid a hand on my shoulder. "I'm proud of you, Sid."

"What the hell am I doing, Rachel?"

"You're moving forward. Getting on with your life." She walked back behind the counter and waited on an older lady in a bright red coat.

I sank down in my chair and gripped the coffee cup. I found myself mumbling in a voice that barely rose above a whisper. "What the hell am I doing?"

Thirteen

Elizabeth Landers was outside pruning shrubs when I pulled into her driveway. She wore jeans with a powder blue jacket and matching wool cap and was kneeling on a square piece of beige carpeting. I parked the Subaru and walked up to her. With a snap of her pruning shears, she stood and greeted me with a warm smile. Her blue eyes twinkled.

"Hello, Sidney. I'm anxious to hear your report. Let's go inside for some tea, shall we?"

I followed her into the house through a sliding glass door that took us through an arctic entryway, a laundry room, and finally into a spacious, sunlit kitchen that I had little doubt would make a small restauranteur envious. Oak cabinets lined the walls. The hardwood floor gleamed under bright, happy lighting. In the middle of the room there was a huge island with oak stools lining each side. Elizabeth gestured toward them. "Please, make yourself at home while I brew some tea."

I eased myself onto a stool and watched her fill a copper kettle with tap water, set it on the stove, and light a flame underneath. She took a small greenish tin box and two brown mugs from a cabinet and placed them on the counter.

"You should find something in here that suits you."

Picking through the packages, I selected an exotic red tea that had been one of Molly's favorites. I tore open the package and placed the bag in my mug.

After five minutes of chitchat about gardening and the coming of winter, a plume of steam rose from the kettle. She filled the mugs and sat down on a stool directly across from me. "So, what have you been up to?"

"I went to see Paula Abernathy at Aurora."

Elizabeth shook her head. "What Harvey saw in her is a mystery to me."

I shrugged. "She seems capable enough."

"Perhaps, though I find her choice of office attire highly inappropriate."

I decided to change the subject. "She did provide one little nugget of information."

"Oh?"

"She said Harvey was acting out of sorts the last couple of weeks. Scared, maybe."

Elizabeth raised an eyebrow. "Scared of what?"

"She didn't know."

She sighed. "That doesn't really help us much."

"She noticed the change in his behavior when he returned from a fishing trip to Skilak Lake with Joe."

Her eyes widened. "I remember that trip. Come to think of it, he didn't speak a word after he got back that night. What do you suppose it means?"

"I'm not sure."

That wasn't entirely true. I had a hunch something had happened between Joe and Harvey on the Skilak Lake trip, although I had no idea what that might be. I saw no point in upsetting her until I had something more definite.

I gripped my cup, embracing its warmth. "I also talked to Joe yesterday."

"He told me. I gather you two didn't hit it off."

"I find Joe to be an acquired taste. Guess I need more time."

"He's not everyone's cup of tea, I'll grant you, but he's been a dear friend. And since Harvey's death, he's been my rock."

"His collection of stuffed heads is most impressive, especially that big moose hanging over the fireplace in his den." I managed to hide any trace of sarcasm.

She shuddered visibly. "I was shocked when he showed it to

me. I asked him how he could stand to look at the thing knowing it had killed Tom."

"What did he say?"

"He doesn't see it the same way. He thinks Tom would have
wanted him to keep it."

"And you?"

"I thought it was disgusting and told him so."

"He obviously cares for you a great deal, Elizabeth."

"Yes, I know." She smiled faintly and took her first tentative
sip. "I'm not blind to the fact that he would like for us to be a
couple."

"Have you considered it?"

She fixed me with a piercing gaze. "Do you find the idea
that odious?"

In a word, yes.

"Let's just say he's a little rough around the edges."

"That would be a good way to put it. Joe is intelligent, loyal,
and protective. I find those qualities admirable in a man. Heaven
knows I'm not getting any younger. A woman has to consider
her options."

"He got upset when I asked him about Tom. Any idea why?"

She stared at her cup as though weighing how much to tell
me. "Joe has always been a bit jealous of Tom."

"Because of you?"

"Partly that, but also jealous of Tom's popularity, his reputation as a lady's man. Jealous of how it all came so easy to him.
So, yes, there was some resentment there. Certainly not unheard
of in even the closest friendships."

I blew away the steam from my mug. "Did they ever come
to blows?"

Her eyes shot up from her tea. "What have you heard?"

"Paula mentioned something about an altercation."

She sighed. "It's true, they fought once. Harvey told me
about it. The three of them were on a fishing trip. Tom and I

had been married maybe ten years at that point. Evidently they were laughing and drinking and having a good time when my name came up. Just like that, Joe was all over Tom, throwing punches. Harvey said he went crazy, screaming that Tom didn't really love me. That I was nothing more than his trophy wife."

"Sounds like jealousy talking—with a shot of alcohol mixed in."

"No doubt. I heard that kind of talk back in high school after Tom and I got together." She blushed. "Tom had many rivals."

"Who won the fight?"

Her face glowed with satisfaction. "Joe may be big and strong, but Tom boxed in college. Harvey told me he cleaned Joe's clock."

I would have paid a hundred bucks to see that one.

I said, "Well, were you?"

"What?"

"Tom's trophy wife?"

Her face clouded over like a spring thunderstorm. I waited while she sipped some tea, set her cup down, and rose from her stool. "Come with me. I want to show you something."

Oh boy. Another trip down memory lane.

She led me down a wide set of stairs and into a brightly lit room with a view of the inlet. One wall consisted of a built-in bookcase; another was empty save for the mounted head of a massive brown bear. Two plush reclining chairs, each with its own ornate reading lamp, were positioned in front of a stone fireplace. In one corner stood a roll-top desk with a matching oak chair. Elizabeth made a sweeping gesture with her arm that reminded me of Vanna White on *Wheel of Fortune*. "This was Tom's personal study. It's just as it was when he died."

I glanced around. The quiet elegance of the room stood in stark contrast to Joe Meacham's man cave.

Elizabeth spoke to me in her peculiarly soothing yet authoritative voice. "I brought you here to show you what Tom meant to me and what I meant to him."

I followed her gaze to the fireplace mantel and the wall above it. Nearly every inch of both was covered with framed photographs of the couple. Everything from their wedding portrait to photographs of fishing and hunting trips they'd gone on together. I honed in on one of her stooped over a Dall sheep, smiling proudly and cradling a rifle. I leaned in for a better look.

"Surprised?" she said, scooting up next to me.

"Nothing about you surprises me, Elizabeth."

"We had such a great time on that trip." She turned to me. "I shared in his wilderness adventures, to the extent my job allowed." She stood there, lost in thought. I asked her what she was thinking.

"Tom dreamed of building a wilderness lodge on Lake Clark. Our plan was to operate it together." Her face saddened and she fell silent.

Molly and I had dreams too, albeit more modest ones. We talked of someday building a home on the hill overlooking Kachemak Bay near Homer. It was a dream that never came true.

I said, "Who knows? Maybe someday you'll have that lodge."

"Perhaps." She smiled faintly and moved to one of the recliners, upon which sat a plain cardboard box. She lifted its lid and gestured inside. "These are Tom's personal effects. The medical examiner's office sent them to me after he died. I've barely touched them in two years. Have a look, if you like. There's not that much here."

I peered inside. The contents consisted of what you might find on the average man's person: wallet, pocketknife, Bic lighter, wristwatch, that sort of thing.

She reached into the bottom and latched onto something small and shiny. "Tom's wedding band." Cradling it in her palm, she said, "Want to hear a funny story?"

"Sure."

"When Tom proposed to me, he made me promise that once we put our wedding rings on our fingers we'd never take them off. Not ever. Well, at breakfast the morning after our wedding night I noticed his ring finger was purple and puffy. The metal had apparently reacted with the oil on his skin, making his fingers swell and cutting off the circulation. From then on, Tom had to take his ring off each night and put it on again in the morning. It embarrassed him to no end that he had to break our promise."

She returned the ring to the box every bit as gently as she'd taken it out and sorted through the remainder of its contents. I watched her touch each item in turn as if she were touching Tom himself. I recalled the day I had received my own little box of memories. It wasn't much, just a few things that had been in Molly's pockets.

Elizabeth's hand lightly touched my arm. "I don't have to tell you, do I? We've both lost someone we love."

I suddenly felt awkward and exposed. "You've gone through it twice in two years. I can't even begin to imagine how that feels."

She shook her head. "You men. Always so strong and stoic." Her brow curled in sadness. "I've lost two partners that I loved dearly. Both died violently. Both ended up on the medical examiner's table. How strange is that?"

I nodded in agreement.

She closed the box. "Shall we finish our tea?"

I motioned toward the door. "After you."

We returned to the breakfast bar and I sipped some of my now-lukewarm tea. Elizabeth drank from her cup. "So, what will you do now?"

"Keep investigating. Concentrate on what we know."

"And what do we know?"

"I think Harvey's suicide has something to do with Tom's death."

"You really think so?"

"Nothing else makes any sense."

"You think something happened on that hunt?"

"I do."

"The troopers said it was an accident. They did an autopsy."

"They've been wrong before. Anyway, it's just a theory. "

She set her cup down slowly. "You're asking me to revisit Tom's death. Sidney, I'm afraid. I've lost two wonderful men. I don't know how much more I can take."

Elizabeth was a remarkably strong woman, but everyone has a breaking point. I was living proof of that.

"I'm just the hired help, Elizabeth. I'll stop right now if you want me to." Even as the words fell out of me I knew I didn't want to stop. Just a few days ago nothing would have suited me better than to hole up in my apartment with a case of Corona, but now something was clawing around inside me, trying to get out.

"No, don't stop. But I wish to be informed as soon as there are any developments. Is that understood?"

I nodded and set down my cup. "I should be going."

She lifted her teacup and held it. "Where to next?"

"The one place I always go when I have a question. The public library."

Fourteen

A fifteen-minute drive put me in Midtown, where the main branch of the public library is located. I wanted to know more about Tom's death, and the best way to do that was to track down the newspaper clippings. Those were stored on microfilm in the library.

I thought about asking my new reporter friend Maria to pull the news clips from the *Daily News* morgue files but thought better of it. Somehow it didn't seem right hitting her up for a favor prior to our first date.

As I neared my destination another thought occurred to me. I plucked my cell phone out of my shirt and punched in a number. A female voice answered on the second ring.

"Lois," I said. "It's Sid."

"Wow, Sid. Twice in one week. To what do I owe this honor?"

Guilt clawed at me. I felt like a fair-weather friend. "What can I say? I'm a schmuck."

"Don't beat yourself up." After a pause, she said, "What gives?"

"Remember a case involving a hunter killed by a moose a few years back?"

"Sure. It's not every day somebody gets whacked by a moose."

"Did you work the case?"

"I was on duty when the troopers brought him in. Why?"

"Remember anything unusual about it?"

"Other than the obvious, no. Hey, what's this about?"

"I'd rather not talk about it over the phone. Can you meet me for lunch tomorrow and bring a copy of the autopsy report?"

"Trying to get your old friend in trouble?"

"It's not like you haven't done it before," I reminded her. When she didn't reply, I said, "Come on, Lois. I'll buy."

I heard a chuckle. "How could I pass up a rare opportunity like that? But you have to tell me what this is about, okay?"

"I promise. Meet me at the Mighty Moose at noon."

"Will do," she said, adding, "Still living with that ornery cat?"

"I'm telling her you said that."

"Narc," she said.

The Z.J. Loussac Library is an imposing post-modern structure named after a former Anchorage mayor. I pulled into a tree-lined parking lot adjacent to a circular reflecting pool and eased out of the Subaru in time to see a row of art-deco tubes resembling a giant mangled pipe organ spit geysers of water into the air. The September sun kissed my face and I felt a rare sense of peace. Nearby, young couples strolled through the manicured landscape, some stopping to gaze at the water display, others relaxing on the grassy slope encircling the library on two sides.

Molly loved to come and sit by the fountain and throw popcorn at the gaggles of Canada geese that seemed to be everywhere. I deftly navigated a minefield of goose droppings and climbed a long flight of stairs leading to the second level entrance. There a stern-looking man cast in bronze and gripping a floppy jacket and cane greeted me. I didn't need to read the inscription to know the man was William Seward, the guy who negotiated the purchase of Alaska from Russia for seven million dollars. At the time some called it "Seward's Folly" but now, except for a handful of diehards who believe Alaska should secede from the union, most folks think Seward had a pretty good idea.

With a nod to Bill, I stepped inside and took the stairs to the third level, where the Alaska Section is housed in a special wing of the library. Getting there requires a side trip down a long hallway lined with landscape paintings and an elevator ride to the level below. I found myself in a large circular room with shelves lining the outer wall and a series of tables in the center. Behind a small metal desk sat a middle-aged woman with a thick crop of black hair atop a kindly oval face. A wooden nameplate pinned to her plain white blouse read: Margaret White - Research Library.

"How may I help you?" she said with an I'm-here-to-help smile.

"I'd like to see the Anchorage Daily News microfilm for the month of September, two years ago."

"Of course. Right this way." She led me to a series of gray metal filing cabinets with rows of wide, shallow drawers, each marked with a series of dates. She reached for one without hesitation and after a quick scan placed her hands on a small box. She turned to me. "Do you know how to use our film readers?"

"You bet. I have an advanced degree in microfilm reading."

She smiled and led me to a side room containing a row the film readers. Margaret handed me the box of film as I sat down. "Let me know if you need anything else," she said as she strolled away.

I loaded the film reel into the machine and soon had the spool spinning with a whirring sound reminiscent of Molly's blender. It took only a few minutes to find what I was looking for. The story was on the front page, just as Elizabeth had said. The headline, spanning the full width of the newspaper, appeared below the fold.

Moose Attack Proves Fatal to Hunter

By Maria Maldonado

A moose attack in a remote area north of Dillingham has left one man dead, his family and two fellow hunters in shock, and state troopers and game officials scrambling to piece together what happened.

Anchorage resident Thomas "Tom" Landers, 38,

was fatally wounded Tuesday about five miles from the party's hunting camp, located on a tributary of the Nushagak River, some 60 miles upriver from Dillingham, according to a brief statement released by state troopers.

Landers and fellow Anchorage residents Harvey Kahill and Joseph Meacham were stalking a bull moose when the animal charged Landers, the statement said. Mr. Meacham told troopers he fired at the animal and killed it, but not before the animal fatally wounded Landers.

Due to the remoteness of the site, troopers and the medical examiner arrived by floatplane several hours after the attack and found Landers at the campsite with massive trauma to the head and chest. He was pronounced dead at the scene and flown to the hospital in Dillingham. From there he was taken to Anchorage, where an autopsy will be performed on Monday.

Sgt. Art McMullen, a spokesman for the state troopers, told the *Daily News*, "Mr. Landers appears to have been the victim of a tragic accident. We are withholding further comment pending completion of an autopsy."

Clint Fargas, a state game biologist, told the *Daily News*, "Bull moose are belligerent and prone to attack during the fall rut. Alaska's hunters should use caution when approaching these animals."

In a strange twist to this tragic story, the moose that killed Landers was reportedly the largest ever taken in Alaska.

There are an estimated 120,000 moose in the state. Although moose can be aggressive during the rut, fatal attacks are rare. Five years ago, a University of Alaska student was fatally attacked as he emerged from a building on the Anchorage campus.

Mr. Landers is a graduate of McKinley High School and the University of Alaska, Anchorage. He was well known in Anchorage hunting circles. Mr. Meacham operates a local guide service. Mr. Kahill owns Aurora Electronics Supply in Anchorage.

Mr. Landers is survived by his wife, Elizabeth. Calls to the Landers residence late last night were not returned. Neither were calls to the homes of Mr. Meacham or Mr. Kahill.

I read the article a second time and made a few notes. The name Clint Fargas caught my eye. Recalling my conversation with Maria, I was willing to bet a steak dinner at Sullivan's that Fargas had been her source at Fish and Game. I decided to make interviewing the game biologist my next order of business. I printed out a copy of the article before rewinding the film reel and returning it to the drawer.

Ten minutes later I was sitting in the driver's seat, gazing at the spouting fountain. I leaned back in the seat and closed my eyes. Three hunting buddies on their annual safari, presumably having a good time, encounter one very pissed-off bull moose. I'd heard stories of fatal moose attacks, enough to know what an irate moose can do. I imagined the animal rushing out of the brush in a murderous rage, barreling like a locomotive. That moose was not going to stop coming.

If that's what really happened.

Fifteen

I grabbed lunch at a fast food joint in Midtown and headed downtown to the Boney Courthouse. The domestic violence section is on the first floor. A thin girl with straight blond hair and a long face greeted me with an ambivalent "May I help you?"

"I'd like to see a file, please." I handed her a slip of paper with the file number and she disappeared into a back room, returning in less than a minute with a cherry red folder. Inside it were a dozen pages bound with metal fasteners. On the right side of the folder, at the back, I found a multi-page document entitled *Request for Domestic Violence Protective Order* filled out in shaky but legible handwriting. I thumbed past the first few pages to Janet Foster's statement. It was short and to the point. Her boyfriend Joe Meacham had gotten mad, threatened to kill her, and thrown her across the room. That was it. She'd sought the protective order late on a Friday night, which means she probably waited for who knows how long before seeing the magistrate, who then issued a protective order that night.

I flipped to the last page of the form and found what I wanted most: Janet Foster's address and phone number. I jotted down the information and scanned the rest of the file. Two days after Janet filed the papers, an APD officer served Meacham with an order forbidding him to go near Foster's home or workplace.

That must have pissed him off.

The judge's order was good for thirty days. He'd also scheduled a follow-up hearing, at which time Foster could appear and request a long-term order lasting anywhere from ninety days to a year. Meacham also had the right to appear at that hearing and explain why a long-term order was not warranted. It came as no surprise that neither one of them showed up. A typical scenario is: a wife or girlfriend is knocked around, gets pissed off, and files a protective order. Later, she experiences a remarkably sudden change of heart after reconciling with her abuser and never goes back to court. I believe they call it the circle of violence.

I left the courthouse wanting very badly to talk to Janet Foster. But my next order of business was Clint Fargas, whom I strongly suspected had been Maria Maldonado's source when she was looking into Tom Landers' death.

Fargas is a familiar face in Anchorage. Whenever a bear is loose in the city or a moose decides to take a nap on someone's front porch, Clint is the guy the TV stations called for on-air comments. I knew him casually, having interviewed him on a couple of fish and game cases I'd worked for the public defender.

I reached Clint at his office. We exchanged pleasantries, then I asked if he could spare a few minutes to discuss a case I was working on. He told me to come on over.

As I cruised south on C Street, my thoughts turned to my pending date with Maria. I found myself attracted to her, feelings I hadn't allowed myself to have until now. And why not? Molly had been gone for almost a year. Surely, she would want me to get on with my life, as Rachel never stopped reminding me.

So why am I feeling so damn guilty?

The tennis match between my lizard brain and my conscience dragged on for the ten minutes it took me to get to a sprawling two-story brown and green office building. I parked and breezed through the entrance. A minute later a tanned, athletic man with a thick head of tousled jet-black hair and a bushy mustache to match greeted me with a firm handshake. Somewhere in his early fifties, he was dressed casually in jeans and a tan sports shirt. He retreated behind his desk and waved me into a chair.

After some small talk, he said, "How can I help you?"

"I'm investigating the death of Tom Landers."

He scratched his chin. "That one's not ringing a bell for me."

"He was killed while on a moose hunt near Dillingham two years ago."

Clint raised an eyebrow. "I remember it now. A terrible accident."

"So they say."

The eyebrow arched again. "You don't agree?"

"I'm not sure if I agree or not."

The biologist leaned forward, resting his forearms on the desk. "What exactly is your interest in this matter, Sidney?"

"His widow hired me."

"Hired you to do what exactly? He died two years ago."

I paused, choosing my words carefully. "There are aspects of the case we have only recently become aware of. I understand that the nature of the injuries led some to question the account given by the two survivors."

Clint fidgeted in his chair. "I don't know what to tell you. I wasn't at the scene."

"I'm told the troopers consulted you on the matter."

"The lead investigator showed me some photographs. He wanted my opinion about them."

"Photographs of what, exactly?"

"The man's injuries. They were official photographs, so I'm not sure I can discuss what was in them in any detail."

"The newspaper reported that there was massive trauma to the face and chest. Is that consistent with what you saw in the photos?"

"It is."

"You've seen injuries caused by moose on other occasions?"

"Many times."

I looked him dead in the eye. "Were the injuries you saw in those photos consistent with a moose attack?"

He rubbed his hands together, as though he were warming

them over a campfire. "You're putting me in an uncomfortable position."

Tell me. You know you want to.

"Clint, my client's lost both a husband and a fiancé. She could use some closure."

"It's not that simple. You're asking me to second guess the state troopers and the medical examiner."

I sighed. "Look, I'm not trying to get anyone fired. This isn't going to be on television."

The relaxed game biologist of a few minutes ago was gone. The furrows on his brow and forehead reminded me of a topographic map. He wanted to tell me what he thought. He hated playing the pencil-pushing bureaucrat who did what he was told. I felt for the guy.

"Understand, Sidney, I retire in two years. If it came out that I contradicted the official report, they could make those last two years very uncomfortable."

I moved closer, lowering my voice. "I'll leave your name out of it, Clint. You have my word. I was never here."

He looked at me intently. I held his gaze. "If I'm ever asked about this, I'll deny it. Understand?"

I nodded.

Clint leaned back in his chair and took a deep breath. "The investigator brought me some photographs to look at. It wasn't exactly official. More like, 'Hey, look what I got to work on.' More or less bragging about it."

"Was it Trooper Pendleton?"

Reluctantly he nodded. "I've worked with him on a couple of cases. Don't really know him that well. A bit arrogant, if you ask me. I looked at the photos and, well, they didn't look right."

"How do you mean?"

"I'm quite familiar with moose behavior and I've seen injuries caused by moose. Moose attack with their front hooves, resulting in cuts and abrasions, sometimes deep lacerations."

"You mean there wouldn't be blunt force trauma?"

"Well, there could be that also." He paused, searching for the right words. "Look, I don't know what happened out there. For all I know, those guys were telling the truth. What I'm saying is, the wounds I saw didn't look right. For starters, I expected to see more deep cuts and lacerations from the hooves. Those types of injuries were not present in the photos I saw. I told Pendleton as much."

"What did he say?"

"He brushed it off. Said he'd already written his report and wasn't going to change it."

"How did you feel about that?"

Clint shrugged. "It's not like I was expecting him to turn summersaults or anything just because I looked at a few photos. He had access to things I didn't. I guess what I'm saying is, I didn't lose any sleep over it."

I rose from my chair and we shook hands. "I've taken up enough of your time, Clint. Thanks for your candor."

He came around his desk and met me at the door. "I think there's something you should know."

"What's that?"

"Pendleton's star is on the rise." His voice was almost a whisper. "Word is, he's set to head up AST's investigation division come first of the year. Like I told you, if I'm ever asked about it, I'll deny I ever spoke to you."

"I guess Pendleton proves the rule. Every man rises to the level of his incompetence."

He frowned. "Watch yourself, Sidney."

Sixteen

It was almost four o'clock when I got back to my apartment. Priscilla greeted me in her usual fashion and returned to her throne. I stared at its scuffed wood surface and wondered if there ever comes a time when the heart stops aching.

Not now. You've got work to do.

I dialed Janet Foster's number. On the first ring, a sterile female voice intoned, "We're sorry, the number you have dialed—"

I pulled out the laptop and checked the usual links but came up empty. I made a mental note to follow up on the address tomorrow. I doubted she still lived there, but it was worth checking out.

I sat on the edge of the bed, stripped off my shoes, socks, and shirt, and loped to the fridge. I had my fingers wrapped around the door handle when the phone rang. Ordinarily, I'd let the machine pick up, or at least check caller ID first, but this time I reached for it without a moment's thought.

An all-too-familiar female voice said, "Hi, Sidney. How are you?"

It was Barbara. I hadn't spoken to Molly's sister since the funeral. Though we'd never been particularly close, she'd been a frequent visitor to our home, as we had been to hers. Their personalities were like night and day, despite a strong physical resemblance between them. I thought of Barb as a dark-haired version of Molly. Barb and her husband Bob lived in Palmer, a quaint little town forty miles north of Anchorage, notable for being the site of the Alaska State Fair. Palmer was founded as a social experiment. In 1935, President Roosevelt offered two hundred families from Minnesota, Wisconsin, and Michigan the chance to start fresh, shipped them to Alaska, and gave them forty acres each. About a hundred of these mostly Scandinavian transplants stuck it out beyond the first year, and their descendants still populate the area.

It was in part because Barb already lived in Alaska that I'd been able to persuade Molly to move to Anchorage from Tucson, Arizona, where she was born and raised. We'd met while I was on a special teaching assignment at the Army Intelligence School at Fort Huachuca, a 90-minute drive to the south. Nestled at the foot of the Huachuca Mountains in southeastern Arizona, it had been an old cavalry post from which soldiers hunted the famed Indian leader Geronimo.

One hot summer day I decided to go horseback riding in the hills near the fort, as I often did in my spare time. I was descending a hill on a narrow trail, riding a rather lackadaisical Appaloosa, when I spotted two female riders coming up the hill toward me, riding side by side. One, a tall redhead, sat atop a buckskin mare. And then there was Molly, riding a spirited little Pinto. Her long, honey blond locks reminded me of spun gold. She wore tight jeans and reddish-brown leather boots with frills along the top. With the sun at her back, the white cotton blouse she wore seemed to glow. With some difficulty, she reigned in the Pinto.

"Mind moving aside so we can pass?" she said.

"I don't think so."

She frowned. "You don't think so?"

"You're coming up the hill. It would be easier for you to move aside."

She frowned. "Now you listen to me, you—"

"I haven't seen you around. You can't be an instructor."

"My father, Colonel Leonard, teaches at the intelligence school. I'm here visiting."

"I know your father well. He's a good man." I sat there staring at her, knowing I had to see her again. "Tell you what. I'll move aside if you let me buy you dinner."

She looked like she'd just as soon ride roughshod over my prone body as have dinner with me. Before she could respond, her friend pulled her aside and they conferred. Finally, the blonde, smiling triumphantly, said, "Okay, we'll move aside if you buy us *both* dinner."

And that was that. By the time the evening was over I was in love with her. I don't remember anything about her friend—not her name, what she was wearing, nothing.

I didn't want to talk to Barbara. Although she'd tried to call me on a number of occasions since the funeral, I could never bring myself to return her calls. I gulped down a lung full of air and said, "Hi, Barb. How's life in the big city?"

"I see you're still quick with the wisecracks, my dear brother-in-law."

"One of my many talents." I let a moment pass and then I said, "It really is good to hear from you after all these months. How have you been?" It *was* good to hear from her. It made me feel connected to Molly somehow.

"I'm all right. It's been a pain the last few weeks though. You know how it is during the fair. We get overrun with lunatics. I'll be glad when it's over and little old Palmer can go back to sleep."

"I'll bet." During the annual twelve-day event, thousands of folks converge on the fairgrounds just south of town, making driving in the area a nightmare for Palmerites.

"Did you go this year?" she wanted to know. I wondered how long she was going to keep up with the small talk before she got around to unloading on me about Molly.

"Didn't see much point. You can see only so many cows, horses, and corn dogs."

There was a pause—the awkward pause of awkward pauses. I tried to cough out a few words but nothing came.

Finally, she said, "It's been nine months now, Sidney. Why

haven't you called me? It would have been nice to hear something from you."

Guilt pecked at my brain. I shuffled my feet. "Yeah, well, I really didn't know what to say. It's not the kind of situation I was expecting to have to deal with."

"You think it's been easy for me? She was your wife, but she was my sister. It would have been nice to have someone to . . . to lean on. She was the only family I had left."

Gentle sobbing came over the line. When it stopped I said, "I was never one for dealing with emotional stuff. You of all people know that."

"Only too well. As did Molly."

"What's that supposed to mean?"

"You know damn well what it means. You're an emotional cinder block. The poor woman was in agony. She needed you. And how did you respond to her cries for help? You either went on surveillance or went fishing!"

Note to self: Check caller ID before picking up phone.

I started to reply but she cut me off, her voice choking with bitterness. "Do you think it was easy for her, dealing with your emotional distance? Do you have any idea how many times she came to me crying because she was unable to talk to you about something?"

I mumbled, "No."

"Of course you don't. You were too busy working on your cases. If you'd spent half as much time talking to Molly as you did to your clients, Molly—"

"Would still be alive?"

There was a long, agonizing moment of dead dog silence. At the end of it she said, "This is not where I wanted to go with this call."

"Well, since we're already there, you might as well say it. You think she'd still be alive if I'd been there for her."

There was an audible sigh. "I didn't say that."

"You didn't have to."

"Sidney, I'm not going to do this with you. I called to see how you're doing."

"I'm fine. Terrific."

"Are you working?"

I gulped down some deep breaths. "As a matter of fact, I'm working on a case right now."

"Care to talk about it?" I knew what she was doing. Barbara had always been the diplomat of the family.

"It's a domestic case. I'm not really at liberty to discuss it. Client confidentiality and all that." I laced my words with a little more sarcasm than intended.

"Of course," she replied curtly. "Have you been to see Dr. Rundle yet?"

That stung. I'd forgotten she'd recommended I see a psychiatrist.

"As a matter of fact, I have."

"Are you still seeing him?"

My irritation was mounting. I didn't appreciate being reminded to go see a shrink, especially by Barbara. This was starting to feel more like an interrogation than a social call. "I didn't find him particularly helpful. I haven't been back."

"He can help you if you let him. Promise me you'll give it another try."

"I promise I'll think about it."

"You're not going to see him, are you?"

"What do you want from me?"

"I want you to take responsibility."

"You're acting like my mother. You always have."

"I'll never understand what my sister saw in you."

"When you figure it out, let me know."

"Damn you, Sidney. Everything is a joke with you. The feelings of others be damned! You dragged poor Molly up to Alaska and kept her here when you knew she hated it—"

"Don't give me that. She loved it here."

"Like hell she did. *You* loved it here. She was miserable, but she stayed because she loved you, although I can't imagine why."

Before I could respond I heard the dreaded *click*.

I said, to no one, "Neither can I."

Seventeen

Barbara's voice was still ringing in my ears when I heard a rapping at the door. *Now what?* I yanked it open, expecting an insurance salesman.

"Hello, Sidney."

It was Paula Abernathy. I couldn't help but stare at Harvey's former business partner. She wore a beige miniskirt that was even shorter than the dress she'd worn in her office, a royal blue sweater that clung to her body like saran wrap, and black, strappy heels. There was nothing subtle about this gal.

But something was different. Gone was the confident, sassy woman I'd met two days before. The Paula standing before me now appeared troubled, vulnerable.

"Paula. Are you all right?"

"May I come in?" Her voice trembled.

I was in no mood for this. I was tired and in dire need of a drink. But being Sidney Reed, rescuer of distressed damsels, I waved her inside.

"I know it's terribly awkward my coming here like this, but I have to talk to you."

As she approached I was engulfed in a halo of perfume. I led her to the couch. Priscilla glanced up from the rocker, displaying mild interest. The same could not be said for me—or rather, the part of me controlled by my lizard brain. As Paula settled into the couch, her miniskirt rode up her thighs, leaving most of her toned and tanned legs on display. I managed to shift my gaze to her sad eyes.

"Okay, Paula," I said, weariness in my voice, "what's wrong? Has something happened?"

"What's wrong?" She spat out the words. "That Landers bitch fired me, that's what's wrong!"

Elizabeth apparently hadn't wasted any time exercising her newly acquired authority over Aurora Electronics, and Paula wasn't taking the news well. But why come to see me? For that matter, how had she found me?

Paula gently sobbed. Not having any tissue in the house, I wondered if I should offer her a napkin or something. No, what I needed to do was get her calmed down.

"Can I get you a drink? Wine, perhaps?"

She looked up, her eyes moist. "That would be sweet of you, Sidney."

In the kitchen, I found an old bottle of cheap chardonnay in a cupboard. A little more fumbling turned up a corkscrew. I popped the cork and hesitated.

Knock off the knight-in-shining-armor crap and get rid of her.

I gripped the neck of the wine bottle, recalling the many evenings Molly and I had relaxed on the couch with glasses of chardonnay. Good stuff, not this junk. I hadn't become a beer drinker until Molly died. I hadn't become a lot of things until Molly died.

I filled two moose mugs with wine and returned to the couch. Paula nodded her appreciation and took a sip.

"All right, Paula. Tell me what happened."

She gripped the mug tightly between her fingers. "Elizabeth called this afternoon and asked me to come to her house. She said she wanted to talk about the business. That should have been my first clue. I mean, why would she want to talk to me?" She paused to sip some more wine. "So I drive out there to her big fancy home in the hills and, low and behold, Joe Meacham is there, too."

"Really?" The thought of Elizabeth and Joe together made me cringe, but then I remembered my client telling me how supportive Joe had become since Harvey's death.

"Uh huh," Paula said before emptying her mug. "If you ask me, they're more than just friends."

Paula is nothing if not savvy in the ways of love.

"Anyway, she told me Harvey had left her the business, and as she's telling me this, Joe has this shit-eating grin on his face and I'm thinking to myself—I'm so screwed." She held up her mug. "Would you be a dear and bring me another?" For emphasis, she batted her product-laden eyelashes. "Please?"

With a nod, I took both our mugs and headed for the kitchen. I'd hoped the wine would calm her. Instead, it was having an entirely different effect. I refilled our mugs and settled back into the couch.

"You were saying?"

Paula frowned. "She tells me she's decided to make some changes at Aurora. While she appreciates my many years with the company, my services will no longer be required." Her grip on the mug tightened. "Eighteen years I worked my ass off for that man. Now some prissy bitch comes along and thinks she can just toss me out the door. That woman's got another thing coming, believe you me!"

I didn't speak. I was focused on the half-filled mug bobbing around on the end of her arm.

Rachel's gonna be pissed if she finds a wine stain on the carpet.

I motioned toward the mug. "Why don't you drink this down. It'll calm your nerves."

She did as she was told. Lowering her glass, her eyes moistened. "What am I going to do?" she whimpered. "Aurora is my life!" Her whimper turned into a full-on cry.

Reluctantly, I slid over and placed a hand on her shoulder. "It's not the end of the world, Paula. You're a smart and talented woman. There are dozens of companies that would give their eyeteeth to have someone with your skill set." I didn't think companies had eyeteeth, but then again I was pretty sure Paula wasn't interested in correcting my grammar.

She dialed her crying back to a whimper. "You . . . really think so?"

"I know so. To hell with Aurora Electronics. Think of this as an opportunity to move on to bigger and better things."

Christ, I sound like a ten-dollar-an-hour motivational speaker.

Paula leaned into me, her industrial-strength perfume overpowering. "You're a good man, Sidney. I can tell you love helping other people. It's what you're good at."

No, what I'm good at is fucking up my life.

She scooted so close I could feel her warm breath on me. "Do you mind if I ask you a question, Sidney?"

I took a long sip of wine. "Fire away."

Paula freed one hand from her mug and laid it gently on my thigh. I felt her bare leg press into mine. "Do you find me attractive?"

My pulse quickened. It felt like someone had spun the dial on my thermostat. The typical male in me told me I could have her if I wanted. I remembered what Kenny G had said about Paula and her husband having an "understanding." No doubt it had been many years since hubby had fulfilled her needs, if he ever had. It didn't matter. I wasn't going to be the one filling them.

I lifted her hand off my knee and placed it on hers. "I told you, Paula, I'm . . . I'm spoken for."

"Ah yes, I remember. Priscilla, isn't it? She must be quite a woman."

I glanced at the rocker, where Priscilla was snoozing like an old man. "She certainly is." I gulped down the rest of my wine and stood up. Paula stared at me, eyes on fire, the sadness and anger and whatever else she'd been feeling replaced by pure, old-fashioned lust. Trying to sound casual, I said, "How did you find me?"

She paused in mid-sip. "Easy peasy. I had a paralegal friend look you up."

I inhaled deeply and shuffled to the bookcase. Picking up

Molly's framed photograph, I drew my fingers across the glass and recalled how after a long surveillance she would complain teasingly that I must have been on Flattop Mountain making out with a secret lover. That always made me smile. The idea of being unfaithful to her was unthinkable.

I recalled what Barbara had said to me not half an hour earlier: *She was miserable, but she stayed because she loved you.* Maybe she was right. Maybe I'd been so wrapped up in my work that I'd been oblivious to Molly's feelings. I returned the picture to its rightful place as the effects of the wine kicked in. Corona worked remarkably well at softening my guilt; cheap chardonnay, not so much. Woozy and wistful, I rested my head on the top of the bookcase and closed my eyes.

Paula sidled up next to me and said, "She's beautiful." Her expression had changed from one of lust to sympathy—or was it pity? "She's not coming back, is she?"

I felt the blood drain from my face. "No, she's not."

Paula leaned in and kissed me on the cheek. "Neither am I."

She set her mug on the coffee table and gathered up her purse. She stood there looking at me, head tilted sadly, once more in control if a bit unsteady on her feet.

"Goodbye, Sidney. I hope you find what you're looking for."

I lifted a hand in a half-wave. "See you around, Paula."

She smiled weakly. "You're a good man, Sidney Reed, but there's a sadness in you that will destroy you if you let it."

Strappy heels tapping, she turned and walked out the door.

Eighteen

It was almost 10 a.m. when I woke, a bit nauseous but thankful my night had been nightmare-free. I stumbled into the living room, where Priscilla was mewing up a storm. A glance at her food dish revealed the source of her anxiety. Under her watchful eye, I scooped a cupful of pebble-sized chunks from a large purple bag and plunked them into the dish. After cleaning out her litter box I jumped in the shower and soaked for twenty minutes, feeling halfway recharged by the time I toweled off. Half an hour later I was facing Rachel Saint George and ordering a tall mocha. She greeted me with her usual charm and grace.

"Jesus, Sid. You look like death warmed over."

"Can't you be nice?"

"I am being nice. Too much warm beer?"

"No. The beer was cold, as was my fried bologna sandwich."

Rachel shook her head. "You've really got to take better care of yourself."

"Tell me about it." Mocha in hand, I snatched Friday morning's paper off the counter and trudged over to my favorite table by the window. I took a sip and perused the paper, hoping to kill some time until my lunch date with Lois. One piece in particular caught my eye. Maria Maldonado had a byline on a story about law enforcement on the Hillside. Apparently, the city wanted to raise the property taxes of residents there to cover the cost of police protection. Seeing her name got me thinking about our date tomorrow night. As the reality of it sank in, I felt an odd mix of panic and guilt. Was I really ready for this?

A familiar voice interrupted my thoughts. I glanced up and

saw Lois Dosier standing in line at the counter. I got behind her in line and we made small talk. She carried a burgundy notepad under her arm with the M.E. office's logo stamped in gold lettering on the front. She ordered a half-sandwich, half-soup combo and I asked for a turkey on wheat. Five minutes later we were seated at the wobbly table by the window.

I watched her attack a steaming bowl of clam chowder. "Are you going to make me wait while you finish that?"

She paused, spoon in mid-transit. "Can't you let me enjoy my lunch?"

"By all means, enjoy."

"A little anxious, are we?" She set her spoon on her plate and handed me the notebook. "Here. If you're not going to eat, at least chew on this. I don't think you'll find it all that tasty."

I opened the pad to find a document consisting of about a dozen typed pages stapled together.

I looked at her. "Thanks."

"Don't mention it."

"You've read it?"

She nodded. "Reviewed the file, too."

It occurred to me I was acting like a kid on his first day of school so I set the report aside and picked up my sandwich. I saw her smile as I bit into my turkey, which I found irritating.

"Give me the short version," I said with my mouth half full.

She slurped down a spoonful of chowder. "What we have here is a bad case of man-meets-moose. Massive trauma to the head and chest. Face caved in. Severe internal injuries. Most of his ribs were broken. Collapsed lung. The guy was a real mess."

Her description produced an involuntary shudder. I tried to appear nonchalant when I said, "Could the injuries have been caused by human hands?"

She looked at me like I was on crazy pills. "Based on the photos I saw? Not likely." She paused to down another spoonful of chowder. "I know where you're going with this, Sherlock. I can see the wheels turning in that over-inflated head of yours. Three buddies are out in the woods in the middle of nowhere. Two of them beat the third one to death and claim it was an accident. The only problem is, the facts do not support that conclusion. The injuries were clearly consistent with a moose attack. The M.E. looked at the wounds, noted the presence of animal hair, and reviewed the trooper's report. This evidence also corroborates the statements of the guy's two hunting buddies. So, unless you can figure out how a man can gain eight hundred pounds and grow antlers, the case shall remain closed."

"Hey, don't blow a gasket. I was curious, that's all."

We both fell silent, munching away.

Lois glanced at me. "I don't suppose any of this has anything to do with the suicide out at McHugh Creek?"

"You could say that. My client is the widow of the moose attack victim. After his death, she hooked up with Harvey Kahill, the McHugh Creek suicide. They were to be married."

She shook her head. "Talk about unlucky in love. Does she think her ex-husband was murdered, or is that your own private fantasy?"

"She just wants to know why Harvey ended it all. I happen to think there's a connection between Harvey's suicide and Tom's death. I thought maybe the autopsy report would shed some light."

"Jesus, Sidney. Give it a rest, will you?" Her mouth formed a thin line. "Not everything is a conspiracy."

"What's that supposed to mean?"

"You know damn well what it means."

I did know. In my grief, I had refused to believe Molly had committed suicide, so I paid a visit to the medical examiner and gave him a piece of my mind—a rather unstable piece. "Yeah, well, I'd just been through hell."

"Sidney, you accused my boss of covering up your wife's murder. He had every right to throw you out of his office."

"That was a bad time for me, okay? And you could have backed me up."

"You were way out of line and you know it."

Of course she was right. With a half-turn of my head, I looked outside. A pair of smartly dressed young women hurried along, overcoats pulled tightly around them. I turned back as my friend popped a potato chip into her mouth. "I know what it looks like, but this is not about Molly. It's about finding some closure for my client."

"If you say so."

She finished off her sandwich and washed it down with a swig of ice tea. "All I can tell you is, Tom Landers was not murdered."

I picked at the remains of my own sandwich, keeping quiet.

She glanced up. "I have this feeling you're not going to leave this alone."

I didn't reply to that.

Lois set her plate aside. "I shouldn't be telling you this, but you'll probably find out anyway."

"Find out what?"

"Pendleton was the lead investigator."

I didn't want to let on that I already knew, so I said, "And you expect me to have faith in the findings?"

Lois shot me a look. "I know you didn't just impugn the integrity of the medical examiner's office . . . again."

"Sorry. That came out wrong."

"Look," she said, "I'm the last person in the world you'll find defending Pendleton, but the facts are the facts. You're looking for something that isn't there."

"Still, I'd feel better if the investigation had been conducted by a real investigator."

"Pendleton wouldn't be my first choice, but he's not that bad." Lois dabbed her mouth with a napkin. "Perhaps someday you'll tell me how the feud between you two got started."

I smiled thinly. "Perhaps."

"By the way, we've missed you at the investigator association meetings."

"I'll bet."

She smiled. "What's the matter, Sid? Don't like us anymore?"

I stiffened. "One of the things I've always liked about you, Lois, is that you don't interfere in my private life."

She stared thoughtfully into her glass and then looked at me. "We've known each other a long time. I consider you my friend, and as your friend I'm telling you, you need to come to terms with Molly's death. Find some closure. Look at you. You're holed up in that tiny apartment all day. I'll bet you're drinking like a fish. You can't go on living like this."

I let her words percolate awhile. I was suddenly aware of the steady din of voices from the lunchtime crowd that filled the place. Lois gulped her ice tea.

"Let me ask you something," I said. "Ever had to see a shrink?"

She set her glass down. "You mean like ordered to go?"

"No. I mean, ever need help dealing with something you couldn't handle on your own?"

"Are you kidding? After I divorced Ronnie I was in counseling for two years. It was like being deprogrammed from a cult. The only positive thing about it was, Uncle Sam picked up the tab. Witnessing what happened to Molly would be enough to make anyone crazy. As if that wasn't enough, you see some dude off himself. I'd be ready for the funny farm."

"You're saying I should see someone?"

"If you can afford to pay for the sessions, why not? Heck, if it were up to me, we'd all be in therapy."

"I just never thought much of shrinks. They're so—"

"Stop making excuses and fix the problem." She stood and pulled on her jacket. "I gotta go. Unlike some people, I work for a living." Lois picked up her notebook, minus the autopsy report. "You didn't get that from me."

I watched her walk briskly out the door and turned my gaze

to the slim report in front of me. Lois was a good investigator, with instincts to match, and those instincts told her I had nothing to be suspicious about.

Then again, she didn't know what I knew.

Nineteen

I tossed the Landers autopsy report on the coffee table and made a mental to-do list. Two leads that came immediately to mind were Bud Branigan, Joe Meacham's former business partner, and Janet Foster, the woman who'd filed a domestic violence restraining order against Joe. I also wanted another crack at Joe Meacham, but decided that could wait.

Reluctantly, I added the psychiatrist, Dr. Rundle, to my list.

Bud Branigan was listed in the white pages at an address in South Anchorage. Five minutes later I was behind the wheel of the Subaru weaving through downtown traffic. I suddenly found myself transported back to the days when I was a working P.I. That feeling of unraveling a problem and making it right again, or trying to. It felt damn good.

The fifteen-minute drive down the Seward Highway was a pleasant one. The Chugach Mountains, which ring the city, were painted with a fresh coat of termination dust. Chubby gray clouds danced between the peaks, threatening to dump more. I guessed that Anchorage's first "official" snowfall was likely just days away now. Halfway there, I caught a glimpse of Flattop Mountain. Molly and I had often gone there to hike.

It was almost 1 p.m. when I pulled into a U-shaped driveway fronting a well-kept tan split-level home. A tall, lean man in his late 30s wearing a red plaid shirt and faded jeans was unloading firewood from an older red Chevy pickup that, like many Alaskan vehicles, had seen better days. He stopped what he was doing as I approached. I introduced myself and we shook hands.

"Mr. Branigan, I'm here about Harvey Kahill."

"I'm not much for formality. Call me Bud."

"You bet," I said, pleased at his directness.

"Follow me." Bud preferred to keep moving while we talked, so I followed him back to his truck. "I was sorry to hear about Harvey's death. He was a good guy." He glanced at me. "What's this about?"

I told him of my client's need for closure after Harvey's death.

He said, "I need to set this wood next to the house so I can load the truck with gear. Tomorrow I start my moose hunt."

I walked beside him cradling chunks of wood in my arms. Bud spoke with a faint southern drawl and had an easy way about him that I liked. He placed an armful of kindling on the woodpile. "Do you hunt, Sidney?"

"Used to. I sort of gave it up." I did a mental rewind to a few years back. I had packed the truck and was ready to head out to Glennallen with my friend Mel Denton for a weekend of grouse hunting. I was standing by the front door, about to recite my usual goodbyes. Molly stood a few feet away, arms folded. She had those little horizontal lines running across her forehead.

I said, "Why don't you come with me this time?"

"You know how I feel about hunting. And besides, I'd just be sitting around the cabin all day."

"You'll just be sitting around here all day."

She glared at me and I shrunk to the height of our shag carpet.

"I didn't mean it that way," I said.

"Yes, you did." She turned toward the kitchen. "Have a good time, Sidney."

I stood by the door, watching as she left the room.

Branigan's voice rose from somewhere in the distance. "Now, them boys were always after a trophy, a big head to stick on their wall. That never interested me. Got nothing against it, mind you. To each his own." He leaned a little closer, smiling. "Between you and me, I think them fellers collect those big heads to compensate for another kind of head bein' too small, if you know what I mean."

We both laughed.

"Tell me about Joe Meacham. I understand you two were in business together."

He nodded. "For a while. We went halves in a guiding business. He had this plan all worked out. Made it sound pretty appealing, like we could make a fortune. I stuck it out for a year, then ended the partnership."

"What happened?"

Bud's jaw tightened. "It dawned on me pretty quick that Joe was looking for somebody to do his dirty work for him. Run errands, that sort of thing. That's not a partnership in my book."

"How did you guys meet?"

"We were classmates at McKinley."

"Were you close?"

"I'd call it a casual friendship. We played varsity football so we were teammates, but we didn't hang out together."

Bud and I hoisted another armful of wood from the truck.

"What else can you tell me about him?"

Bud thought for a moment. "Helluva football player. Strong as an ox, too. Ever seen him?"

I nodded.

"Then you know what I'm talking about. He put a couple of kids in the hospital."

"I guess the man didn't know his own strength."

"Oh, he knew. When a football coach tells you to ease up, you know you've got a problem. And Coach Letterman wasn't what you'd call a wimp." Bud paused. "He used to say, 'Football's not a contact sport, it's a collision sport.'"

"He must've been a great coach."

"And then some. Won more championships than any other coach in state history."

"What about Tom Landers?"

"Good guy. Team captain. Natural-born leader. How does he figure in this?"

"He doesn't strike me as the type who would buddy up to Joe."

Bud set his bundle of wood on the growing stack and thought for a moment. "You wouldn't think so. They were different as night and day. Tom was outgoing. Made friends easily. Joe was quiet and tended to keep to himself, and yet they seemed to get along just fine. I know they went snow machining together quite a bit. For whatever reason, Joe looked up to Tom and maybe Tom thought of himself as a mentor to Joe. That's my take on it, anyway."

As we strolled back to his truck he continued. "They had a common interest in hunting. Harvey, too. Those three were always talking guns, ammo, or hunting." He looked at me and grinned. "And girls, of course. Yeah, they were pretty tight, those three."

We both collected armfuls of wood and started back toward the woodpile.

"Ever see them argue?"

"Sure. Same thing most guys argue about—girls. One girl in particular." He stopped and grinned. "As a matter of fact, it was your client."

"Elizabeth Landers?"

"That's her." He leaned his arm on the tailgate. "New transfer. Real knockout. Half the guys in school chased after her, Joe included. He could be charming when he wanted to be. That didn't last long once she met Tom."

"You don't say?"

"Couple of times Joe got a little too friendly with her to suit Tom and Tom let him know it."

"They ever come to blows?"

"Not that I know of, although I saw them go nose to nose a few times." Bud snapped his fingers. "That reminds me. There was this one kid, Ricky Favor. Wide receiver. Nice kid. A real clown, too. He made it his mission in life to pull a fast one on everyone on the team. Didn't care who—you might say he was an equal opportunity practical joker. We all warned him to stay away from Joe, but that didn't stop Ricky. I don't remember what Ricky did, but one day after practice Joe grabbed hold of Ricky in the locker room. Now, mind you, Ricky's no midget. He's maybe six one, one eighty, or thereabouts. Well, Joe picked him up by his jersey and shook him like a rag doll without any more effort than it would take you or me to shake a kitten. That's how powerful that man is. Well, Joe shoved him up against the locker so hard it left a dent, then dropped him on the floor like a bag of cement. When Joe walked outta that locker room, you coulda heard a pin drop."

Investigators are blessed with a natural curiosity. The really good ones have an instinct; a sixth sense, if you will. It's what sets them apart from the pack. I used to have it. When something didn't smell right, the hairs on the back of my neck would stand up. Now, as I listened to Bud talk about Joe, those little hairs were driving me crazy.

We arrived at the woodpile with the last of the wood and stacked it nice and neat.

"Appreciate the help," he said as he walked me to the Subaru. "Anything else you wanna ask me, Sidney?"

I gazed toward the Chugach Mountains and sucked fresh air into my lungs. "I don't know. Think you'll get a moose this year?"

"Sure," he smiled. "Freezer needs fillin'." Then his smile disappeared. "It was a helluva thing how Tom died. A really bad deal. Now Harvey's dead, too. Two good friends dead in two years. Figure the odds on that one."

I didn't answer—math was never my strong suit. As we shook hands, he said, "I sure hope you figure this out, Sidney."

"I will," I replied, and slid behind the wheel.

On the drive back I didn't look at the Chugach Mountains. I was too busy thinking about what Bud had said. The same three words kept clanging in my head like a church bell.

Figure the odds.

Twenty

At the Tudor Road exit I turned east toward the mountains. Janet Foster's last known address, plucked from Joe Meacham's court file, was on the east side of town. Muldoon, named after the main street running through it, is a loose conglomeration of trailer parks, low-rent apartments, and bars. I doubted Foster still lived there, but I hoped to at least get a lead as to where she'd gone.

The building was a dingy yellow eight-plex with one of those long metal mailboxes bolted to the front of the building. The name "Foster" was scrawled in magic marker on a faded white tag under box number eight—encouraging, but by no means proof she still lived here. Seeing the front door propped open with a softball-sized rock, I slipped through the entrance and into a small foyer permeated with the stench of carpet mildew. I climbed to the top floor and, through the gloom, located Apartment 8. My knuckles rapped hard against a gray metal door.

It opened slowly and I stood facing a woman of about thirty with scraggly, shoulder-length auburn hair. She was nervous and gaunt and clutched a cigarette in her bony right hand, and I knew I was looking at Janet Foster. I decided the badge might help so I took it out and showed her.

"Janet, my name is Sidney Reed. I'm a private investigator. I'd like to talk to you about Joe Meacham. May I come in?" She leaned closer to the badge, studying it. "You a cop?"

"No, ma'am."

"You're not working for him, are you?" Apprehension coursed through her voice like static.

"No, ma'am."

Her pale-green eyes darted nervously. Her head bobbed out of sight and I heard a chain rattle. The door swung open.

"Well, come in." She led me down a hallway that widened into a kitchen and living room. The place reeked of cigarette smoke. She helped herself to one of three rickety metal chairs gathered around a tiny scuffed white dining table. I sat down on one of them and studied her as she fidgeted in her chair. A thin stream of chalky gray smoke rose lazily from the cigarette notched between her outstretched fingers.

"Thank you for talking with me, Janet."

She took a long drag on her cigarette and flicked the ashes into a Styrofoam cup already populated with a small colony of spent butts. Her hand shook. Dark circles framed her eyes and her skin was mottled and leathery. She looked much older than her thirty years. Everything about her screamed meth head.

"You're here about Joe? What's he done?"

"Tell me about the restraining order you filed against him."

Her stare was cold, vacant. "If you read the file, you know the bastard tried to kill me."

"I want to know what's not in the file."

"Why do you care?"

"I don't, but I have a client who does."

"Who's your client?"

"I'd rather not say."

"Well, Sidney, tell your client to watch their ass. Joe has a nasty temper."

"I'll let them know." I waited, letting her inhale some more nicotine and relax a bit. "Were you with him long?"

Her eyes followed the smoke trail upward. "About a year, I guess. Met him in a bar in Spenard. I was waiting tables." She chuckled to herself. "I was in a little better shape back then. Hell, I was pretty damn hot."

I didn't doubt it. Janet had fallen a long way in two years. Meth will do that to you.

She studied me for a reaction. Seeing none, she said, "He was tall and rather handsome, it was a slow night, and he tipped well. We chatted until closing time, then I let him take me home."

"Tell me about the restraining order."

Her lips trembled in time to the twitching of her hand. "Wouldn't you know it? The damn cop who took my report was the same one who nabbed me on a prostitution rap two years before. How's that for luck, mister detective?"

I didn't speak.

"Know what he told me? He said, 'Hey Janet, you still working Spenard?' That motherfucker."

"He didn't believe you were assaulted?"

She shot me a withering look. "Ah, no." She stared at the table and flicked some more ash toward the cup. Most of it missed. "Yeah, I turned tricks for a while. You bet your ass I did. When my ex dumped me, I was left with two little pie holes to feed. I did whatever I could to survive. Damn right I did."

I listened.

"Turns out, it was one trick too many. The last one was a cop. I pled out and my public defender got me probation. Next thing I know, a social worker's knocking at my door." She stared at me hard, her lower lip quivering. "You have kids, Sidney?"

I shook my head. Molly and I had talked about it, but that was as far as it got.

She stabbed her cigarette butt into the cup and fought back tears. "They took my kids away and stuck them in foster care."

The floodgates opened, her tears pouring out like summer rain. Spotting a roll of paper towels on the kitchen counter, I got up and tore off a square, handed it to her, and sat back down. She dabbed her eyes and I waited for her to collect herself and look at me.

"Is that when you started using?"

She sniffed and nodded. "Once Joe was out of the picture I let this guy named Jerry move in with me. It was good at first.

He bought me things, treated me nice. With my kids gone, I needed someone nice, you know? When I told him about my kids, he said he would help me get them back if I helped him. Next thing I know we're cooking meth in a trailer up in Willow. One day he says, 'Hey baby, you gotta try this shit.' Like a dumb ass, I did. He got busted, of course. Got himself a cell down in Seward and I got probation again. Managed to hold onto this dump though. Thank God for the Dividend."

Through the efforts of former Alaska governor and bush pilot Jay Hammond, every man, woman, and child in Alaska gets a check each year from the state, their share of the oil revenues paid to the state by oil companies. Hammond was a crafty old bush rat who understood the oil would run out some day, leaving Alaskans high and dry.

"Did Joe ever offer to help you out?"

"You're kidding, right? He's supposedly a hotshot bush pilot, but when it came to helping me out he never had two nickels to rub together. Oh, he brought me groceries a couple of times, after bitching that I never had any food in the house. But it was never what you'd call a whirlwind romance. It wasn't that kind of a thing." She stared at the cup as if expecting Joe to leap from the ashes. "Anyway, he had a thing for some bitch named Elizabeth."

"Oh?"

"Yeah, a real schoolboy crush. She was all he ever talked about except for hunting and fishing. It was always Liz this or Liz that. One day I got fed up with it and said, who's this Liz bitch you're so hot for, anyway? Big mistake. Next thing I know I'm flying across the room."

She motioned toward a faded green chair in the corner. "See that chair? That's where I started out." She turned and pointed at the stove. "See that dent down there near the bottom?"

The indentation was small but unmistakable.

"That's where I ended up. I had a big fat goose egg for a week.

I remember lying there, all dazed, with this fucking giant looking down at me, and he says, 'If you ever mention her name again, I'll fucking kill you.' Those were his exact words, swear to God." She paused to light up another cigarette and exhaled a long plume of dirty white smoke. "Naturally I did like the man said."

"That when you filed the restraining order?"

She shook her head. "Damn sure wanted to. He apologized, got all nicey-nicey for a while, so I didn't. My counselor calls it the circle of violence." With raised bony fingers she put air quotes around "circle of violence."

"You mentioned he had a thing for Elizabeth."

"More like an obsession."

"Why didn't he do something about it? Why wasn't he with her?"

She blew a perfect smoke ring toward the light fixture above the table, her lips curling into a satisfied grin. "The lady was married. And get this: her husband was a friend of his."

Tom Landers.

"Not long after that, he went on a hunting trip with a couple of his buddies."

"Did you meet them?"

She puffed and smirked. "I wasn't good enough for Joe's friends. I was just his whore."

"And then?"

"When he got back he told me a moose killed his friend. Turns out the dead guy was the one married to that Liz chick. After he tells me that, he says he can't see me anymore, have a nice life, honey. That really set me off. I started yelling at him, throwing shit. He just laughed. That was the last time I ever saw him." She sucked on her cigarette until the tip glowed cherry red.

I said, "Let me guess. You went to court and filed the restraining order for the earlier incident, only you made out like it just happened."

Her nostrils flared. "Serves the bastard right for walking out on me! Didn't matter anyway. I never went back to court, so the whole thing got dropped."

I watched as she pulled another cigarette from a pack in her shirt pocket, lit it, and took a long drag. "Funny thing is, he didn't seem that upset about his friend dyin'."

"You don't say?"

She leaned across the table. "Wanna know what I think? I think he was happy that moose killed his friend. With him gone, Joe could have Liz all to himself."

I rose from my chair. I'd gotten what I came for. It was time to move on. "Thank you for your time, Janet."

She stared at me blankly. "My momma wants me to come back to Missouri and live with her. Offered to buy me a plane ticket. Believe me, I'd love to get out of this shit hole, but I can't. Not without my kids." She looked me dead in the eye. "You think the state will give me my kids back, Sidney?"

How many clients like Janet had there been over the years? How many had, like her, been sucked into a vortex of drugs and addiction? The only thing keeping this woman alive was the hope of someday seeing her kids again. Barring a miracle, that wasn't going to happen, but I wasn't going to be the one to take that hope away from her. Not today. I patted her hand and said, "Get yourself clean, Janet, and maybe you will."

That started her crying all over again.

I went back to my car and sat there thinking about Joe Meacham. We all have a side we seldom show. Joe had a violent side, a side he'd managed to keep hidden from Elizabeth for twenty years. But some people saw it. People like Bud Branigan and Janet Foster. Now, more than ever, I wanted to confront Joe about Tom Landers.

There was just one thing I had to do first.

Twenty-one

At twenty minutes past three, I parked the Subaru outside a six-story business complex in Midtown. I didn't need to see the building directory to know Dr. Elliot Rundle's office was on the third floor. I stepped onto the elevator, feeling light-headed—dreading this moment even as I conceded its inevitability.

Thirty seconds later I passed through a big brown slab of a door and approached the receptionist, an attractive, twenty-something blonde with braids on each side of her head. She was not the same attractive twenty-something blonde I had seen on my last visit. It's a tough job market.

"Good afternoon, I'm Sidney Reed. And you are—?"

The girl bounced out of her chair. "I'm Melanie."

"Nice to meet you, Melanie. I need to see Dr. Rundle immediately."

She began to leaf through a thick black book. "Do you have an appointment?"

"No, but if you let him know I'm here, I'm sure he will see me."

She closed the book and looked up. "I'm very sorry, Mr. Reed, Dr. Rundle has an appointment coming very soon and—"

"Melanie, I'm going to see Dr. Rundle now, and with any luck I'll be done before his next appointment arrives. Okay?"

She frowned. "Mr. Reed, you cannot—"

I walked past the reception desk and into Rundle's office, where a thin, graying man of about fifty sat behind a huge desk made of cherry. Behind him stood a row of matching bookcases with glass doors. To the right, a plethora of framed diplomas, awards, and signed photographs covered an entire wall while, to my left, a large window offered a panoramic view of downtown Anchorage and Cook Inlet. In the Last Frontier, you can't swing a dead cat without hitting a panoramic view.

He looked up from his desk. "Sidney."

He remembers me.

"Decided to give it another try?"

"I thought I might."

"Very well. Take a seat."

No sooner had I eased into a squeaky leather chair than the door opened and Melanie breezed in, waving her arms in exasperation.

"I'm sorry, Dr. Rundle, he just barged right in!"

The doctor twisted his head in my direction with a look sharp enough to cut glass. "You've got some nerve. I should call the police and have you thrown out."

I said evenly, "We both know you won't do that."

A few years back, Rundle was convinced his wife was cheating on him so he hired me to follow her. After two weeks of round-the-clock surveillance, I came up empty. My gut told me she was faithful. He wasn't convinced. I watched her for two more weeks with the same result. When I gave him my report and my bill—which came to five thousand dollars—he became irate and refused to pay me. I threatened to report him to the state medical board, at which point he got all weepy on me and told me his first wife was killing him with child support payments and the bank was foreclosing on his condo in Maui. He begged me to work with him.

When Molly died, Barbara urged to see someone. That's when I thought of Rundle. It was probably unethical for him to take me on as a patient after I'd been following his wife, but it served both our purposes. We had one session together, but I never went back. Until today, that is.

I said, "I was hoping to pick up where we left off."

Rundle sighed and waved his hand. "That's okay, Melanie. When is my next appointment?"

"Mr. Beasley at three thirty."

Rundle glanced at his watch. "Very well. Let me know the moment he arrives." He shot me an icy stare. "I'm sure this won't take long."

Rundle waited as Melanie closed the door. "All right, Sidney," he said, weariness in his voice. "Give me a minute to pull your file and refresh my recollection." He spun around in his leather-backed chair and opened a lateral file made of polished cherry, bringing to mind John Lennon singing, *Isn't it good, Norwegian Wood.* He plucked out a thin blue file folder and laid it open on his desk.

I fidgeted while he reviewed my file. Peering over the top of silver wire-framed glasses, he said, "Ah, yes. I remember now. Six months ago you stormed out of my office in the middle of our first session. On your way out I believe you called me a snake oil salesman."

"I was going through a rough patch."

"You could have called to make an appointment, Sidney. This is not the DMV. You can't just waltz in here and take a number and expect to be served. I don't work that way."

The Army had taught me a valuable lesson: It's better to beg forgiveness than ask permission. "I really am sorry. If you'll allow me a few minutes of your time, I'll be on my way."

Dr. Rundle leaned forward onto his elbows and massaged his temples with his thumbs. "All right, I'll give you ten minutes, but know this: I will not tolerate any abuse from a patient, verbal or otherwise. Is that understood?"

I nodded.

He eased back in his chair. "So, how may I help you today?"

I took a deep breath. "I walked out of that session realizing I wasn't prepared to deal with what happened. Instead I tried to put it all out of my mind."

"But you couldn't, could you?"

"No."

"You self-medicated."

"Yes."

"You had nightmares."

I nodded.

This guy's good. Arrogant, but good.

Rundle puckered his chin. "What brought you back today?"

"Something . . . happened."

"What happened?"

The lump in my throat felt like a paperweight. "I watched a man blow his brains out pretty much right in front of me."

The doctor slid his glasses back over his ears. "I see."

I gripped the chair. "When that happened, Molly's death came rushing back at me like one big pile of crap."

"And are you ready to talk about what happened to her?"

I released my death grip on the chair and walked over to the window. Puddles of sweat gathered in my armpits.

"I'd just returned from a late-night surveillance. My client was away on business, which left her husband at home to his own devices. She was sure he'd take advantage of her absence and head off somewhere to do God knows what with God knows whom, but in this case the guy never even went out for pizza. I kept up the stakeout until 2 a.m. and then went home."

I turned and caught Rundle glancing at his watch. "As soon as I walked through the door I knew something wasn't right. Don't ask me how. I just knew. Maybe it was the lights. There were lights left on. It wasn't like her to leave them on. Anyway, I walked into the bedroom and . . ."

. . . there she was, lying at the foot of the bed, a halo of blood around her head. Her honey-blond hair was matted with blood and her arms were extended as if reaching for something. Her angelic face looked strangely at peace. Inches from her outstretched right hand lay the revolver I'd bought her for personal protection—how

ironic is that? I turned and vomited on the ornate, jewel-encrusted music box her mother gave her as a wedding gift.

"Sidney?" Rundle was speaking.

"There she was, lying on the floor, dead. Single gunshot to the head." I was shaking. I sucked air into my lungs and settled back into the squeaky leather, my heart pounding in my chest.

He leaned forward. "Good, Sidney. You're finally able to talk about your wife's death." He leaned back in his chair. "When we experience something traumatic, the natural tendency is to bury the memory deep within our subconscious, as a protective measure. I'd say that when you witnessed that fellow's death, those repressed memories bubbled back to the surface."

As I listened, I'd been staring at the leather pencil holder on his desk. Now he was staring at me. "Tell me about the nightmares."

I tried to swallow but felt a knot welling up in my throat. "They start out pleasant enough. Molly and I are hiking or having dinner or watching a movie or something. Everything is good and then suddenly she . . . she's holding a gun and she sticks it in her mouth and then . . ." I bit off the words as I felt my eyes moisten.

No way am I going to show him that.

Rundle sat stone-faced, ever the clinician.

I pulled myself together quickly. "What's really bizarre is, in almost every dream, without exception, she looks at me and says, 'This is your lucky day,' just before she . . . does it. Now that's some weird shit."

He considered what I'd said. "These nightmares are no doubt manifestations of your subconscious mind dealing with the trauma you experienced. Perhaps forcing you to deal with your wife's death even as your conscious mind refuses to."

"Okay."

"Do you feel some responsibility for what happened?"

"You mean, for her death?"

"Yes, for her death. When bad things happen to those we care about, it's not uncommon to feel like it's somehow our fault. Perhaps you feel guilty for failing to prevent it."

My grip on the chair tightened again. "It wasn't supposed to happen. She wasn't supposed to die."

"People die, Sidney. Even those we love most. Oftentimes, there's nothing we can do about it."

"Not her." I wasn't even sure he heard me. It was more of a guttural croaking than coherent speech.

"And you feel you could have prevented it?"

"Could doesn't enter into it, doc. I *should* have prevented it. She used the gun I bought her, for crissake. Hell, she didn't even like guns." My head fell into my open palms.

"Sidney, look at me."

I looked. He was weirdly out of focus.

"Stop blaming yourself."

My jaw went slack. I stared at him. "I can't . . ."

"Yes, you can." Rundle leaned forward. "It wasn't your fault. The sooner you realize that, the sooner you will be able to move on with your life."

Easy for you to say. You weren't kneeling in a pool of her blood.

The air in the room turned to lead. I leaned forward under the weight of it, burying my head in my hands again. I wanted so badly to get those haunting images out of my head. Why can't our brains be more like computers, where we simply hit the delete button and send bad memories into the trash? Through the fog I heard Rundle's voice and lifted my head.

"Sidney, we've only scratched the surface here. I'd like to schedule you for two sessions per month for the time being." Rundle scribbled on his pad.

"That won't be necessary, doc. I think I'm good now."

"Nonsense. This is a process, Sidney. There are no quick fixes."

"Fine," I said sharply. "Set it up."

You can do this, Sidney. You can.

My thoughts drifted to Maria. "Speaking of moving on, I have a date tomorrow night."

Rundle glanced up from his desk. "That's good, Sidney. Socializing is helpful to the healing process."

"Thing is, doc, I'm having second thoughts about it."

"Undoubtedly a case of first-date jitters."

"I don't know . . ."

"Going out will do you a world of good."

"You're probably right."

I stood up and Rundle handed me an appointment slip. "Stick with it, Sidney, and I think you'll find a few months of sessions most beneficial. By the way, have you been working? I recall from our earlier session you were on hiatus."

"I am. Actually, the case I'm working on concerns the suicide I witnessed. The client wants to know why he did it."

A flood of loosely connected thoughts began streaming through my brain like a ticker tape.

He said, "It so happens I've done some consulting work as a forensic psychologist. Do you have any theories?"

The words came quickly. "Yes, a rather wild one. I think the guy who committed suicide had witnessed the murder of his best friend and couldn't bear the guilt of not being able to stop it."

He glanced at his watch. "You don't say?"

I was speaking as much to myself as to Rundle. "Three friends went on a hunting trip. One of them didn't come back. The troopers think that man was killed by a moose, but I think he was murdered."

"Uh huh." Rundle idly twirled the pen he was holding. It looked expensive. Mont Blanc, maybe. My head was spinning, all thoughts of dates and bad dreams replaced by images of a hunting trip gone bad.

"Sidney, are you listening? My next patient is here—"

"Tell me, doc. What makes a man murder his best friend?"

He leaned back in his chair and sighed, flicking the pen open and closed. "Any number of things can drive a man to kill. Greed, hate, power, jealousy, fear, or a combination of these. If there is a woman involved, I'd put my money on jealousy. Ah, Mr. Beasley, please come in."

Melanie had breezed through the door with Mr. Beasley in tow. Rundle waved him into the chair.

Without uttering a word, I slipped out the door.

Twenty-two

I felt a strange sense of relief after opening up to Rundle. Now, as I maneuvered the Subaru through Friday afternoon traffic, I felt something more healing than therapy. A hunch was coalescing into a theory, and it went something like this: Joe Meacham murdered Tom Landers. The motive? Jealousy, fueled by anger. The means? I had no clue. How does one commit a murder and make it look like a moose did it?

It was time for another visit with Joe Meacham. I decided to try and catch him at his floatplane on Lake Hood first thing in the morning.

When I entered my apartment at a quarter past five, my stomach was making gurgling noises, so after pausing to give Priscilla a chin rub I headed for the fridge, cobbled together a ham sandwich, and carried it, along with a bottle of Corona, to the couch. Ten minutes of channel surfing got me nowhere. How could there be so many channels yet nothing worth watching? I switched off the set, finished the sandwich and beer, and drifted into the bedroom, where I executed a belly flop on the bed and thought about what the morning might bring.

I harbored no illusions that Joe was going to blurt out a confession. From what little I knew of him, the man was smart, resourceful, and a master hunter. And if, as I suspected, he was responsible for the death of Tom Landers, he would be a powerful and dangerous adversary. To be perfectly honest, I wasn't at all convinced I was up to the task. A year ago, perhaps. Not anymore.

My thoughts turned to my date with Maria, now less than twenty-four hours away. I had a sudden urge to call her but dismissed it when I realized I only had her number at the paper. I cursed myself for not getting her cell number.

Then a new thought occurred to me. I grabbed my coat and headed out the door.

Joe Meacham's place was shrouded in darkness. I cruised past the house until I found an opening among the trees offering both adequate cover and a reasonably unobstructed view of his property. I eased the Subaru into place and killed the engine. I made myself as comfortable as possible, expecting a lonely night's vigil. Pulling my binoculars out from under the seat, I scanned the house for signs of activity, but saw only narrow slivers of yellow light streaming from a pair of windows.

Moments later the front door burst open and the two hounds from hell I'd met on my first visit exited the house with Joe Meacham in tow. They had the characteristic square head and drooping jowls of the English Mastiff. I figured they weighed two hundred apiece, easy. He tethered the animals to a pair of metal posts in the yard before disappearing around the side of the house, only to emerge less than a minute later lugging a red gas can. Striding up to a mountainous brush pile, he poured the contents of the can onto the stack, struck a match, and tossed it into the pile. With an audible *woomf*, the wood erupted in flames.

Soon the fire found its own rhythm, crackling and splashing Joe's beefy frame with an eerie glow. He turned and walked some fifty feet, stooped down, and wrapped his gorilla arms around a two-foot stump before returning to full height with the huge chunk of wood held tight against his barrel chest. He returned to the burn pile and, in the most impressive display of raw strength I've ever seen, raised the massive stump over his head and smashed it down into the fire, sending sparks rocketing skyward like a swarm of angry fireflies. I lost Meacham in the shroud of smoke and was trying to find him again when a thumping on the driver's side window nearly catapulted me out of my seat. I stared at the face in the window, the mane of wavy, dark hair, those big dark eyes.

Maria Maldonado.

I lowered the window. "Are you out of your mind?"

"Hi, Sidney. Saw you pull in and had to come and say hello."

"Get in before you give us away. And don't slam the door."

She scooted around to the passenger side and slid in beside me, easing the door shut. Settling herself into place, Maria had my full attention. She wore tight blue jeans and a tan sweatshirt under a pale blue windbreaker. Her chestnut tresses shimmered in the moonlight, and within the Subaru's cold interior her smile seemed to radiate its own heat.

She looked at me. "I see you have Joe Meacham under surveillance." A fetching perfume permeated the air around her.

I ignored the remark. "What are you doing here?"

Before she could respond, it dawned on me I hadn't seen her pull up. I glanced around, puzzled. "Where did you park?" She pointed to a clump of bushes about twenty-five yards to my right. Squinting, I spotted a small sub-compact of uncertain color, barely visible among the shadows. "How long have you been sitting there?"

"About an hour." She reached into her coat pocket and pulled out a small pair of binoculars.

Leaning back in my seat, I could feel my temples tighten into knots. It irritated me that I hadn't seen her car when I pulled in. My P.I. skills were getting a bit rusty. I wanted to read her the riot act for putting my stakeout at risk. Except, truth be told, I liked her being there.

"What are you doing here?" I repeated as she trained the binoculars on Joe Meacham.

"Watching a murder suspect, same as you."

"Oh, really?"

"Yep. I smell a story here."

"Yeah, well, I smell trouble. If he sees us—"

"Hold on. He's going inside."

I raised my precision German optics in time to see Joe pass through the front door. "Great. He's going to call the cops."

"Don't be so paranoid, Sidney. It's after dark. I'll bet he's done for the night."

I liked the melody of her voice. The sound of my name when she said it.

"How can you be so sure?"

"If you'd gotten here when I did, you'd have seen him dig up that stump. He just wanted to burn it." She shrugged her shoulders. "Now he's done." She faced forward again, stretching her legs out in front of her, the same way I'd done countless times after hours spent motionless behind the wheel. It helps keep the blood flowing. My eyes roamed over her legs. They were long and slender, and the stretchy blue jeans she wore fit them like a glove. I sighed and tilted my head back against the headrest.

"What are you going to do?" she said.

"Do? Go home and have a beer, I guess."

"That's not what I meant. What are you going to do about Joe Meacham? About the murder of Tom Landers?"

"I never said—"

"Why else would you be here?"

I kept facing forward, but I could feel her eyes on me.

"Sidney?"

I looked at her in the faint light. Her mouth was drawn tight. When I didn't reply, she said, "We can't let him get away with it."

I sat upright in my seat. "It's not like I can waltz up to him and make a citizen's arrest. I have no proof Joe did anything wrong. I have a motive, sure, but that's all. If only I could figure out how he did it, I might have something."

"There must be something we can do." Her voice carried with it the hint of an accent, but I couldn't make it out.

"We?"

She didn't answer.

We stared at the house for several minutes, the only sound our measured breathing. Maria was the first to break the silence.

"Are you excited about our date tomorrow night?"

"I've been thinking about that, Maria. Maybe . . . maybe it's too soon for me."

Her reply came in barely a whisper. "Look at me, Sidney."

I looked. Her eyes, deep and penetrating, were all the more so in the dim light of the Subaru. "You think you're the only human being on this planet who ever lost someone?"

My lips, dry and leathery, parted slightly. I didn't speak.

She turned and stared through the windshield. "We grew up near the Texas border, my mom and brother and me. We were very poor." She paused. When she spoke again, the words came in staccato phrases. "The man she was with . . . was a drug dealer. He did such mean things to us, I can't even . . . One day . . . I was very young . . . she left with him in his car and . . . we never saw her again."

I reached out to touch her forearm. She pulled it away. I realized then that I knew nothing about her. That in focusing on my own troubles I hadn't considered the possibility that she might have some, too. I felt uncomfortable and ashamed.

I cleared the lump from my throat. "Molly had this rocking chair. An old-fashioned wooden one that creaked really bad. It was a big old clunky thing. A real antique. It had belonged to her grandmother. Anyway, when she died, it was the one thing of hers I couldn't bear to let go of. I guess it's my way of keeping her alive."

Maria's face had become lost in the shadows. It was only in the brief flash of light when she shifted her body that I saw her wiping one of her eyes with the back of her hand.

"Why are you telling me this?" she said, sniffling.

"I don't know. Sometimes I just start babbling."

I tried to read her through the shadows, but there were only the dark recesses of her eyes, a glint of soft light illuminating her cheeks. Then I heard the Subaru's door handle rattle, and when she spoke she was as composed as the moment she'd first entered. "It's late. I'll see you tomorrow."

With that, she stepped from the car and walked off into the night.

Twenty-three

I t was almost midnight when I returned home. The drive had been consumed with thoughts of Maria and Joe, each as much a mystery to me as the other. After Maria walked away from my car I'd hung around long enough to see Joe come out to fetch his dogs. Ten minutes later all the lights in the house blinked off. That was my cue to get out of there.

Priscilla hurried to greet me with an affectionate ankle rub, executing a perfect figure eight around my legs. I bent down to give her the chin scratching she craved. She answered with an exuberant meow, purring like an idling Ferrari.

"Care for some chow?"

She knew what that meant. A few moments later she was happily wolfing down chunks of tuna. The queen thus engaged, I shagged a beer from the fridge and settled into the couch. I was still wound up from the evening's events and was counting on a couple of beers to put me in a restful mood. I propped my feet up on the coffee table, clumsily knocking Tom Landers' autopsy report onto the floor. When I bent down to pick it up, it occurred to me that this was my first opportunity to read it since Lois handed it to me earlier in the day. I swigged some beer and began reading.

This one was no different than dozens of others I'd read over the years, describing in dry yet precise scientific language the examination of the human body to determine the cause and manner of death. They are cold, jargon-laced documents. For instance, if an organ or system appears to be what is medically regarded as normal, it is said to be "unremarkable." So why can't they just say "normal?"

The report described Tom's injuries in explicit detail. I slogged through it somewhat mechanically until one tidbit caught my eye. In a section describing the wounds to the left side of Tom's face, the writer noted

> . . . a series of five parallel marks beginning two centimeters below the external auditory meatus and extending approximately 8 centimeters to the anterior portion of the zygomatic bone. Each mark is approximately .5 centimeters in width and .5 centimeters equidistant from the next, varying in length from .7 to 2.2 centimeters (anterior to posterior). These marks were visible as faint red lines under gross observation, but were measurable and photographed using an alternate light source. It is concluded that these marks were made ante mortem by an object striking the victim and leaving a corresponding mark on the skin. This object could not be identified.

Translation: Before Tom died, something struck him on the left side of the face and left a series of five parallel red marks on his skin. What could have left such marks? Had Pendleton or anyone else made any effort to identify their source? His report would answer those questions, but I didn't have access to it and was unlikely to get it. Evidently the marks had not bothered the medical examiner because he concluded Tom's injuries were "consistent with an attack by a large ungulate." I tossed the report on the coffee table with a sigh.

My gut told me Tom's death had not been an accident, but it takes more than a gut feeling to prove murder. Harvey's suicide note wasn't nearly enough. I did have a motive: Joe had been obsessed with Elizabeth since high school and was jealous of Tom. Given his propensity for violence, I reasoned that something had happened on that hunting trip to push him over the edge. Joe most likely forced Harvey to help him cover it up.

Unable to live with the guilt, Harvey put a gun in his mouth and fired. It was one helluva theory, anyway.

Who was I kidding? It was going to take a lot more than solving the Landers/Kahill case to make my life whole again. The sad truth was, I had to come to terms with Molly's death if I hoped to become a functioning human again. Barb had reminded me of that, in her own quaint way.

I pulled myself up from the couch and headed for the bedroom closet, in search of the scattered remains of my life. From the moment I'd found Molly's lifeless body lying on the bedroom floor of our home, I knew I could no longer live there. Not in the same house where we'd laughed and cried and made love. Not where she had died.

Against the advice of my realtor, I had put the house up for sale, and in one of those oh-by-the-way conversations, he told me that if someone is killed in your home and you decide to sell it, you have to disclose that fact to potential buyers.

I tried to imagine the conversation: *You folks are going to love this place. Three bedrooms, two baths, two-car garage, central air, nice neighborhood. You'll especially love the master bedroom. Huge walk-in closet, bay windows. Oh, and right there next to the bed is where the missus shot herself . . .*

Given the state disclosure laws and the state of the economy, I took a loss on the place—a big one. Not that I really gave a damn.

Sifting through our accumulated possessions had hurt like hell, but given my mental state at the time I didn't see any benefit in holding on to any of it so I scheduled a moving sale and got rid of everything we owned. Well, almost everything. I kept Molly's rocking chair. And Priscilla. I'd also stuffed some legal papers and others items into a cardboard box and likely would have forgotten about them except for one thing: I remembered Molly kept a diary.

I entered the closet with some trepidation. It was an eight-by-ten walk-in, lined on three walls with stout plyboard shelving and thick wooden dowels beneath them for hanging clothes. A single bare bulb centered in the ceiling provided illumination. Considering the size of my apartment, the closet could qualify as a second bedroom.

The shelves were stacked with an assortment of cardboard boxes, clothing, and other odds and ends. I rummaged around until I found what I was looking for: a large cardboard box labeled Photos & Memorabilia. I wrestled it out of the closet and onto the bed. As I pried open the lid, Priscilla pounced up beside it, curious to see what I was up to.

The box was stuffed to overflowing. Several photo albums lay at the top, taking up half the box. The first album contained photographs from my childhood. There were black and white shots of me swinging on an inner tube hanging from a tree, sitting on an old Ford tractor, and swinging a baseball bat. I moved on to the next album, and then the next. I savored those snapshots of the various stages of my life: growing up in Ohio, my years in the Army, my marriage to, and life with, Molly. As I looked at each individual photograph I could, in my mind's eye, relive the action and emotion behind it, like a video going from pause to play. My stroll down memory lane complete, I set the albums to one side.

Next came a stack of manila envelopes and folders of varying sizes that, on closer examination, contained various civic awards and certificates, such as Molly's humanitarian award from the ASPCA and a Meritorious Service Medal citation from my stint in the Army, the kind of stuff slightly more pretentious people like Dr. Rundle frame and hang on a wall.

Under the envelopes lay a leather-bound book, burgundy in color and roughly the size of a hardback book. On the otherwise bare cover, centered across the bottom and embossed in gold lettering, were the words: PROPERTY OF MOLLY REED. Lifting the book slowly from the box, I sat on the bed and placed it on my lap. I paused and then pulled back the cover and began leafing through the handwritten pages, Molly's flowing script at once recognizable.

Molly's diary.

I closed the cover and thought back to those days. I knew she kept a diary. She'd be curled up in her rocking chair scribbling in it, a wistful look on her face. I'd never asked to read it, believing that a diary is a very private thing, to be read only by its author. Now a part of me wanted to mine those pages for what I imagined were the lost threads of her life, or perhaps even clues to why she'd taken it.

But I wasn't ready to open that door. Not yet. I set the book gently on the nightstand.

I returned to the cardboard box, now nearly empty, a handful of assorted knick-knacks clumped at the bottom. I was about to return the photo albums and papers to the box when I saw a glint of metal. I squinted down into the shadows of the box. There, amid a pile of old keys, paper clips, and whatnot, was a glimmering silver band—Molly's wedding ring.

I lifted it out of the box and held it in my hands. Priscilla, who'd been studying my every move from her resting place at the center of the bed, was there in an instant, sniffing it. Her purring grew louder, her ears cocked to the side, and she rubbed her cheek against it.

How could I forget the day we'd gone to the jewelers to pick out our rings? I thought we'd never leave that place when, finally, she spotted the one she wanted. From then on, she twirled it around her finger incessantly, as if needing to remind herself it was there. "Stop picking at it," I'd tease. She'd smile back and say, "Oh, all right," but then she'd be fiddling with it again moments later.

I suddenly recalled another ring in another box.

Tom's ring.

Stuffing Molly's ring in my pants pocket, I bounded into the living room and snatched up the autopsy report. It only took moments to find what I was looking for, a single paragraph under the heading *Gross Observations.*

> On the ring finger of the left hand, between the second and third knuckle, there is an indentation, one-quarter of an inch in width and extending the full circumference of the finger, lighter in color than the surrounding skin, which is noticeably tanned, consistent with the presence of a wedding band. An examination of the personal effects of the deceased transported with the body confirmed the presence of a gold wedding band of a size and shape consistent with the indentation noted above. The report of investigation states that the ring was not present on the body when found. It is concluded from this that ring was not worn at the time of death.

Elizabeth told me Tom always wore his wedding band, with one important exception: he took it off at night because it made his finger swell up. The implication of that hit me like a bucket of cold water to the face: If Tom was killed in a moose attack during the day, why wasn't he wearing his wedding band at the time of the autopsy?

Adrenalin surged through me like an elixir. I paced the floor, working through a six-pack of Corona, knowing damn well I wasn't going to get any sleep that night.

Twenty-four

I awakened at 9 a.m. Saturday morning with a nasty hangover, though once I'd showered, dressed, and wolfed down a package of cheese crackers salvaged from a kitchen drawer, I was ready to seize the day. It was a pleasant ten-minute drive to the Lake Hood Seaplane Base. The air was crisp and the sun blazed.

The seaplane base at Lake Hood is actually two conjoined lakes—Lake Spenard and Lake Hood—connected by a pair of narrow water lanes, one for takeoffs, the other for taxiing. Dozens of float planes lined the shores of both lakes, their waters constantly churning from the prop wash of arriving and departing aircraft.

It was going on 10 a.m. when I maneuvered the Subaru onto a graveled parking strip skirting the northern shore of Lake Spenard, hoping Joe hadn't already taken flight. Glancing around, I was relieved to see his black Silverado parked next to a corrugated metal shed, next to which a dock jutted finger-like into the lake. His yellow and white de Havilland Beaver bobbed gently at its moorings. The classic bush plane reminded me of a favorite Saturday morning cartoon from my childhood, *Clutch Cargo*.

I strolled over to the shed and peered through a small window, allowing my eyes to adjust to the darkness, when a deep, resonant voice boomed behind me. "Can I help you with something?"

I turned and stood face to chest with Joe Meacham. It was the second time I'd let him sneak up behind me, a habit I wasn't eager to repeat. He wore a tan Carhartt jumpsuit—the preferred working garment of the macho Alaskan male. I didn't realize they came in size GIANT.

"Oh, it's you, Reed," he said. "We're having a big problem around here with theft. Sneaking around like that could get you shot." He could have been joking—he was wearing his signature smirk—but I didn't think so.

"You should carry around a defibrillator, Joe."

He scrunched his face up. "Why is that?"

"Because, if you keep sneaking up on people like that, sooner or later one of them is going to have a heart attack."

Meacham laughed uproariously. Not a chuckle or a guffaw, but an honest-to-goodness belly laugh. He was holding his stomach like jolly old Saint Nick. "That's rich! You make me laugh, Reed. I like that. Seriously, you need to be careful. Alaskans tend to shoot first and sort out the bodies later, if you know what I mean."

I knew what he meant. Alaskans love their guns and don't mind using them if they have to, or even if they don't have to. I'd been involved in more than one case in which a jury acquitted a defendant who'd shot an intruder. The running joke in Alaska is, if you blow away someone outside your home, be sure to drag their body inside before phoning the cops.

"What are you doing here, Reed?"

I gazed out across the lake. "I like to watch the float planes take off." There was some truth to that. It was something Molly and I had often done on lazy Sunday afternoons.

"Lots of people do," he said with a nod. "Lake Hood is the busiest floatplane base in the world."

"I sometimes wish I'd learned to fly." That was true.

Meacham's steely gray eyes bore into me. "Why are you really here?"

"I have a few more questions before I wrap up my investigation. I thought we could chat for a bit."

His slab-like shoulders drooped. "This isn't a good time. I'm starting a ten-day hunt first thing Monday. I was about to take my plane up for a spin to check her out. We'll have to do this another time." He paused, cocking his head. "Unless you'd like to tag along."

I hesitated. As much as I loved airplanes, flying the friendly skies with Joe Meacham ranked on my bucket list somewhere below whale watching with Captain Ahab. On the other hand, it might be my only shot at an interview.

"Well, Reed? I haven't got all day."

I patted the shirt pocket under my jacket to make sure I hadn't forgotten my digital recorder. "Fine by me. Let's go."

With a wave of his catcher's-mitt-sized hand, Meacham motioned for me to get in on the passenger side of the Beaver. I stepped gingerly from the dock onto the float, swung open the door, and hoisted myself into the cabin.

The burly pilot untied the mooring lines and climbed in next to me. I buckled myself in and stared impassively at the dizzying array of levers, knobs, and gauges on the dull gray instrument panel. He flicked a few switches and the engine chugged hesitantly before roaring to life. Moments later he throttled the plane away from the dock and taxied to the middle of the lake. After mumbling something into the mike protruding from his headphones, Meacham eased the throttle forward and we were airborne.

The Beaver banked to the right and in a matter of minutes we were soaring over Cook Inlet. Joe worked the controls with an ease that comes with experience. From all appearances, he was a skilled pilot.

"Ever flown in a one of these babies?" Meacham bellowed above the roar of the engine.

Some of my fondest memories were of the work I'd done in Alaska's bush country, where often the only way in or out was by air. To me, that's the real Alaska. I said, "Once I tagged along on a training flight with the Alaska National Guard."

"Best bush plane ever built." He tapped the wheel for emphasis.

We soared west across Cook Inlet. Glancing out my window I saw clear blue sky in every direction. Below, the sun shimmered off the surface of the inlet thanks to a brisk morning breeze. It was a beautiful day to fly, present company notwithstanding.

Meacham glanced in my direction. "Reed, I was out of line blowing my lid the other day. I think maybe we got off on the wrong foot. I guess Harvey's death has me on edge. I think if you got to know me, we might even be friends. We're both hunters, after all."

The last thing I was expecting from Joe was an apology. However, I saw in it the makings of an opportunity so I said, "I'd like that." I let a few minutes go by and then I said, "I miss my deer hunting days in Ohio and West Virginia. I've often thought it would be fun to try for a moose up here."

"What's stopping you?"

"My late wife didn't believe in hunting. Out of respect for her views, I never went."

"We're all part of the food chain, Reed. The way I figure it, if I don't kill that moose, a wolf or a grizzly will. That's nature."

I found myself agreeing with him. Molly was a diehard environmentalist, a real tree hugger. Some of it had rubbed off on me, though we argued about some things. One of them was hunting.

"Elizabeth seems to be familiar with firearms."

Joe chuckled. "That's an understatement. Did you know she grew up in Eagle?"

"No, I didn't," I said with genuine surprise. Eagle is a small village on the Yukon River, not far from Alaska's eastern border with Canada. "That's what you call a hard way of life."

"Damn sure is. Up there, you learn to shoot like other kids learn to ride a bike."

We buzzed along smoothly under Joe's deft touch and I found myself enjoying the view. He mostly kept silent, attentive to the controls and gauges, no doubt watchful for any indication of a mechanical problem.

I said, "How about you, Joe? Where are you from?"

He cast a sidelong glance in my direction. "Omak. Small town in north-central Washington State."

"What brought you to Alaska?"

"My freshman year in high school I came up to live with my uncle. He's since died."

"How about family?"

"None that matter."

"There must be someone. A brother, perhaps. Maybe a—"

"No one." He half-turned, gray eyes wary. "You seem fascinated with my history, Reed. What about yours?"

"Me?" I glanced out the cabin window and recognized the aptly named Sleeping Lady Mountain, its contours suggesting the shape of a woman in repose. I didn't much like answering questions either, but if it would help him open up, well then, why not? "I was raised on a dairy farm in Ohio. The closest town is so small, it's not even on a map."

"Let me guess. You were a happy child. You spent long hours at the ole fishin' hole, and you were a star on the baseball team."

It was my turn to throw him a cold stare. He was mocking me, and it pissed me off.

Don't let him get to you, Sidney.

I kept my focus on the instrument panel. "Happy? I don't know. When I was thirteen years old I was out helping dad mend fences. He was about a hundred yards or so down the line stringing wire when I saw him go down on his knees, holding his chest. I knew right away what was happening, so I ran to the house and called for an ambulance. He was dead when they got there. That was before everybody had cell phones."

"Tough break, Reed. What did you do then?"

"Mom sold the farm and we moved in with her brother in Columbus. On the day I turned seventeen I enlisted in the Army." I was tired of talking about me, so I half-turned. "Is your old man still around?"

Joe's mouth crimped into a narrow line. "I guess you could say that. He's serving a life sentence in the Washington State Penitentiary at Walla Walla." He turned slowly and looked at me, his expression hard and cynical. "He beat my mom to death with a baseball bat. Is that enough personal history for you, Reed?"

Jesus. No wonder this guy's so fucked up.

We flew in silence for a while as I considered what he'd said. The left wing dipped, signaling that we were veering south toward the northern shore of the Kenai Peninsula. Cook Inlet, with its broad expanse of glimmering water, trailed off to the southwest, where many miles away it meets the Gulf of Alaska. The beauty of the landscape stood in stark contrast to the despair I felt right then. Were the losses he suffered any less rending than mine? After witnessing the deaths of both Molly and Harvey, what was *I* capable of?

Joe's voice rose above the din of these thoughts. "I thought you had more questions for me?"

I sat up straight, realizing I'd almost dozed off. "Yeah, Joe. I wanted to ask you about Skilak Lake."

"What about it?"

"You flew Harvey there for some fishing a few weeks before his death."

"That's right. We hooked some nice rainbows on that trip."

"What did you two talk about?"

"You asked me that already."

"Well, I was hoping for the truth this time."

"I told you the truth. We had a great time on that trip."

"That's funny. I was told Harvey was acting scared when he got back. Why would that be, Joe?"

"How should I know?"

"Maybe because you threatened him?"

"Bullshit. I never threatened anyone."

"That's not what Bud Branigan told me."

"Bud? What's he got to do with this?"

"He told me an interesting story about one of your high school teammates. Ricky Favor."

His eyes darted up and to the left, searching memory.

"Come on, Joe. You remember Ricky. The kid you slammed against a locker."

Joe's face creased in anger. "You seem to be taking a lot of interest in my personal life."

"Just doing my job."

"My ass. What does shit that happened twenty years ago have to do with Harvey?"

Maybe it was his smugness and the way he had Elizabeth thinking he wasn't such a bad guy. Maybe seeing a man blow his brains out makes me cranky. Whatever the reason, my mouth started speaking like it was unattached to my brain.

"How about another blast from the past? Janet Foster."

Joe gripped the stick so tightly his knuckles turned white.

"She says you threw her across the room."

His face contorted in anger. "And you believe her?"

"Yeah, Joe, I do."

Without warning, Meacham jerked the controls to the left and the plane banked wildly in reply. Had I not been belted in I'd have been body-slammed against the door. He glared at me. "Now you listen to me. I want you to stop spying on me. You got that?" He leaned on the stick and the Beaver lurched violently to the right.

"Hey!" I shouted, the first tinge of nausea engulfing me. "You wanna take it easy on the stick?"

"What's the matter? Not used to a little turbulence?"

The plane lurched hard to the left and I felt as if my stomach was being turned inside out. He pointed toward the passenger side window. "Look at that, Reed? Ain't it beautiful?"

Following his gaze, I caught a flash of trees and a hilltop with some snowy patches, blurred like a Leroy Neiman painting.

"Alaska's a beautiful place, but it can be damned unforgiving.

People get lost all the time. One day they're here and the next—poof—they're gone."

When the plane banked yet again, I could have sworn there was a lawn mower working its way through my large intestine. Meacham shoved the throttle forward, launching the Beaver into a steep dive. I imagined someone shoving my bowels into a blender and switching it on. All the while, the man grinned like he'd just won the lottery.

Fuck it. If I'm going to die, I might as well go out swinging.

I leaned toward him and raised my left hand.

"What is it, Reed? Got something funny to tell me?"

The words came slowly, each breath a struggle. "I . . . know . . . what . . . you . . . did . . . asshole."

Meacham turned three shades of purple. "You don't know shit! Tom's death was an accident. The troopers said so."

I forced a weak smile. "Who said . . . anything about . . . Tom?"

He turned a fourth shade of purple and fixed me with a hate-filled stare. The words he spoke turned my blood cold. "Listen to me, you son of a bitch. I don't know what you think you know, but if you keep talking crazy, I'll sue you for defamation. So why don't you crawl back into that rat hole you call an apartment and stay out of my business."

He knows where I live.

As if to emphasis his point, he banked sharply to the right and my stomach executed a perfect summersault. I groaned out the words, "Think I'm . . . gonna be . . . sick," and leaned forward, folding my arms around my midsection. Nearly overcome with nausea, I buried my head in my lap. I wanted to crawl into the baggage compartment and die. I half expected him to boot me out the door in midair. Frankly, I wouldn't have cared if he did. I needed the fresh air.

Time stood still. Aware only of the incessant droning of the plane's engine, I focused every ounce of willpower on retaining the contents of my stomach. After what seemed liked hours, a popping in my ear told me we were descending. A fleeting glance through the windshield revealed the welcome sight of Lake Hood looming ahead. Moments later we touched down, the placid lake and smooth landing belying the hell I'd just gone through.

The Beaver coasted into its berth and Meacham killed the engine. He just sat there, unmoving, while I clutched my stomach and moaned. With his eyes fixed straight ahead and his voice icy cold, he said, "Stay away from Elizabeth and stay away from me . . ." He paused, letting the words hang there like so much black slime. ". . . or I will kill you." With that, he lurched out of the cockpit and set about tying off the lines.

I eased myself out the door and onto the right float, gripping a strut to steady myself. I stood there swaying, hoping to regain my sense of balance—and dignity. Then all the nausea and fear and anxiety came gurgling up as I emptied the contents of my stomach into Lake Hood. A sizeable portion of the soupy mess dribbled onto the float. It was all I could do to keep from falling in after the chunks bobbing on the surface. Still, I kept my balance long enough to hop off the float and stagger up the rise to my car. Behind me, Joe unleashed a fusillade of obscenities. Apparently he'd noticed the vomit on his airplane.

I yanked open the car door and slid behind the wheel, wiping my mouth on my sleeve. The view through my windshield was one I'll never forget: The mountainous figure of Joe Meacham standing beside his airplane, shaking his fist at me and shouting at the top of his lungs, "You threw up on my plane, you son of a bitch!"

I managed a weak smile and reached inside my jacket, my fingers closing thankfully around the digital recorder I'd stuffed in my pocket that morning and which had been recording since I'd first stepped from the car. Gratuitous though it was, I honked the Subaru's horn in farewell as I pulled away from the lake.

Twenty-five

The drive to the Alaska Department of Public Safety Building, headquarters of the Alaska State Troopers, took me all of twenty minutes, but it was agonizing nonetheless. When I parked the car and looked in the mirror of the window visor, I saw a pale reflection of the old Sidney. The events of that morning had left me sallow and drawn. I smelled of dried vomit, having splashed my shoes and pant leg with the vile stuff.

I stepped out of the car and shuffled down a long walkway and through the entrance doors into the main lobby. A portly, dark-haired officer in her mid-30s sat behind a glass barrier.

I said, "I need to see one of your investigators. I have important information about a case."

She buzzed me through a security door without comment. Once inside, I stepped up to her desk and she handed me a clipboard. "Sign in, please. Someone will be with you shortly."

I scrawled my information on the sign-in sheet and took a seat. Coming here was a long shot. Having already ruled Tom's death an accident, the troopers wouldn't look too kindly on having their findings second-guessed, especially by a pain-in-the-ass P.I. I wouldn't have bothered but for the fact that I now had a recording of Joe making some incriminating statements. I wouldn't call it a murder confession exactly, but I'd seen prosecutors go to court with less. Maybe, just maybe, it would prompt a second look at the case.

A few minutes later I cocked my head at the sound of approaching footsteps and groaned. Trooper Barney Pendleton wore a plain gray sweatshirt, faded jeans, and a dour expression.

"Reed. To what do I owe this dishonor?"

I was in no mood for it. "How about we dispense with the unpleasantries. I have some information for you."

He looked me up and down, sniffed the air, and scrunched up his face. "Is that vomit?"

"I was airsick. Look, I have information about a homicide. You want it or not?"

"Fine, let's go to my office. Just don't get any puke on the furniture."

Halfway down a long hallway, he made a right turn into a spacious room filled with plain-looking gray metal desks. Plain-clothed officers occupied half of them. They showed no interest in my presence.

Pendleton gravitated to a desk near a window at the far end of the room and waved me into an empty chair. He leaned back and folded his arms. "Okay, Reed, make it quick. I've got work to do."

I slid into the padded metal chair and met his icy gaze. I had hoped to speak with someone on the weekend shift. Someone other than Pendleton.

Put your big boy pants on, Sidney, and get on with it.

"I'll come straight to the point. Two years ago, you investigated the death of a man named Tom Landers, who was killed on a hunting trip north of Dillingham."

"Yeah, I remember. What about it?"

I sucked in a mouthful of air. "I believe he was murdered."

His eyes grew large. "Come again?"

"I think Joe Meacham killed Landers and made it look like an accident. He admitted as much to me this morning."

"And of course, you have proof of this."

I pulled out my digital recorder and held it up. "I have a recording."

"Let me see that." Pendleton snatched the device out of my hand. After a cursory inspection, he punched the Play button. What came out of the speaker sounded like one of those nature recordings of the ocean, nothing but a rhythmic *whoosh*. Clearing his throat, he pushed Fast Forward, followed by Play. The result was the same: hiss and static. There was no trace of Meacham's voice, or anyone else's, on the machine.

My heart sank in direct proportion to the grin on Pendleton's face. In my eagerness to show off my "evidence," I'd neglected to make sure the machine had been working properly. I had nothing. Zero. I wanted to crawl under his desk and hide.

Way to go, dickhead.

Pendleton said, "If this is your idea of a joke, it's not funny. Of all your lame attempts to embarrass me, Reed, this is the lamest."

"That's not what this is. Okay, I messed up the recording, but I'm telling you, when I confronted Meacham, he threatened me."

"Hold on. You say he threatened you? Did he confess or didn't he?"

"Not in so many words, no. But if you could have heard what I heard—"

"I could have if you hadn't fucked up the recording."

My blood boiled. "I'm telling you this guy murdered Tom Landers and—"

Pendleton cut me off. "What do you want me to do, Reed? Arrest him?"

"Take my statement. Haul his ass in for questioning. Do your job, dammit."

Pendleton's belly laugh filled the room and one by one troopers looked up from their desks and stared at us like zoo animals. Savoring his role as the biggest ape in the room, Pendleton swiveled around to face the man closest to him, a burly cop with a square jaw and crew-cut. "Check it out, Sam. This private dick has solved a murder for us."

"No shit?" Crew-cut replied. "Which one?"

"Remember the hunter killed by a moose couple of years ago near? Reed here says that isn't what happened at all. Says the guy's best friend killed him. Whatcha think of that theory?"

Crew-cut snickered. "Works for me. Bring the guy in, let's book him."

I glared at Pendleton. "Listen, I know we've had our—"

"No, you listen." Pendleton's jaw tightened. "I'm tired of your hunches. If you think this guy killed somebody, bring me some real evidence."

"It doesn't bother you that Meacham and Kahill lied to you about what happened?"

Pendleton's grin faded. "What are you talking about?"

"You read the autopsy report, right?"

"Yeah, I read it. So what?"

"Then surely you noticed Landers wasn't wearing his wedding ring at the time of his death."

"What's your point, Reed?"

"Landers' wife told me he only took his ring off at night, so he couldn't have been killed during the day in a moose attack. Those guys lied to you."

I could see the wheels turning. "That's one helluva deduction, Reed. Don't you think I considered the possibility of foul play?" Pendleton propelled himself over to a row of filing cabinets lining one wall and fished out a tan file folder. He scooted back to his desk, sifted through it, and pulled out two large white envelopes. He set them in front of me. "Have a look at these. Take your time."

I peeled back the flap of the first envelope, labeled *Scene Photos*. Stuffed inside were forty or so color photographs of a campsite, each taken from a slightly different vantage point. One wide-angle shot showed a large tent staked out near the bank of a small creek, complete with a fire pit and camping equipment scattered about. Several large white mesh bags dangled from ropes attached to a tree. I recognized those as game bags hunters used to store meat after field dressing a game animal. The severed head of a moose, with its massive antlers attached, lay on the ground near the camp fire. Various close-ups of the head and antlers showed traces of blood. Fresh snow blanketed the whole scene.

The story of what the troopers saw unfolded in those photos. Tom's body lay sprawled on a camouflage tarpaulin near the tent. His face was horribly bruised and battered, and blood caked his hair and parka. I was glad I'd read the autopsy report in advance; it allowed me to examine the photographs with more care than I otherwise would have. One photo showed the red mark on Tom's left cheek that had been described by the M.E. in agonizing detail. I held it close and squinted, but there was too much dried blood to discern any detail, much less the parallel marks on the skin I'd read about in the report.

I returned to the wide shots of the scene, trying to piece it together. If Meacham's story was to be believed, Tom must have died some distance from the camp, which meant that, before the troopers arrived, Joe and Harvey had dressed out the moose and dragged both their friend's body and the moose carcass back to camp, a chore that would have taken them hours.

I looked up at Pendleton. "Seems odd they would go to the trouble of dressing out the moose after it killed their best friend."

"Not really. We weren't able to get to the scene until the following morning. State law requires hunters to harvest all the meat. They did exactly what they were supposed to."

He was right. Alaska is serious about its game laws.

"How did they report the death?"

"They had a satellite phone."

"What time was the call placed?"

Pendleton, looking annoyed, flipped through the pages in his file. "Eight forty-five p.m."

"He was killed during daylight hours. Why call so late?"

"They told us they carried him back to camp and then went back to carve up the moose. By that time it was late."

I searched through the packet of photos again and eyed Pendleton. "I don't see any shots of the kill site."

Pendleton shrugged. "We looked. Couldn't find the spot."

"You're telling me there were no drag marks leading back to the kill site?"

He picked up one of the photographs of the campsite and stuck it under my nose. "Three inches of snow fell that night. No tracks, Einstein."

I nodded and stuck the scene photo back in the envelope. Setting it aside, I reached for the second envelope, this one marked Autopsy. I'd seen hundreds of autopsy photos, but you never really get used to them. There's something morbidly surreal about seeing a body cut open for inspection. It's eerily reminiscent of the way a hunter dresses out a kill. As I braced myself to look at them, a shiver ran through me.

The sequence of photos was something like this: The removal of Landers' body from a black body bag, lying supine and naked on a stainless-steel table, both before and after the "Y" incision, the peeled-back chest cavity allowing examination of the wounds from the inside. Then comes the really icky part: The incision across the top of the skull and the pulling of the scalp over the face, allowing access to the skull in order to remove the brain for examination.

I flipped through them quickly, not so much because they were uncomfortable to look at, but because I'd read about all of this in the autopsy report. What interested me most were the parallel marks on the left side of Tom's face and knowing what made them. Having come this far, I was disappointed to learn there were only two photographs of the marks. Thankfully, they were visible in sufficient detail that I felt an identification could be made—if there was something to match it to.

I laid the two photographs on his desk and pointed. "What do you make of these marks?"

He gave a quick glance. "We weren't able to identify them."

"Did you even try?"

His face reddened. "I stuck my neck out showing you these

and you question my integrity? I can assure you we did a thorough investigation. Any other questions?"

I set the remaining photos on the desk and gathered my thoughts. I wanted to ask him why he hadn't acted on the concerns raised by Clint Fargas, but couldn't risk violating Clint's trust. I had to let it go.

The room was strangely quiet except for the sound of Pendleton drumming his fingers on the desk. "Well, Reed, can we wrap this up? I'm busy."

"There's more to this story, you know. Joe Meacham has a history of violence and he had a motive to kill Landers."

"What motive?"

"He was jealous of Landers. He wanted his girl."

"Jesus, Reed. Half the men in Anchorage are jealous of somebody. That doesn't make them killers."

My head was starting to hurt. "Meacham killed him. I know it."

"How do you know?"

"I just know."

Pendleton shook his head slowly, like a frustrated father trying to teach his son to hit a baseball. "Okay, fine. You think this Meacham guy murdered Landers? Then answer me this, hotshot: how did he do it?"

I stared at him blankly. I was all out of snappy comebacks.

His lip curled. "Thought so. You see, Reed, you can talk to me all you want about wedding rings and threats and silly hunches. I've got statements from two men at the scene, an autopsy report, a ruling from the state medical examiner, and a moose with the victim's blood on its antlers. If you're so damn sure he was murdered, bring me proof."

Pendleton glanced at his watch. "Hey, this has been loads of fun, but I've gotta run." Rising from his chair, he picked up my recorder and handed it to me. "Have a nice day, Reed. Don't let the door hit you on the way out."

I pocketed the recorder. "Obviously I've wasted my time here."

Pendleton's voice boomed. "This guy's more observant than I thought. You might make a good detective yet, Reed."

His put-down was rewarded with derisive guffaws from his buddies. I could still hear them when I retreated down the hallway. The officer at the desk looked at me like I was a puppy someone had just kicked. "You look like you could use an aspirin."

I said, "You read my mind."

Twenty-six

I sat in my car in the parking lot, staring numbly at the traffic whizzing by on Tudor Road, feeling like I'd just gone ten rounds with Mohammad Ali. Actually, that was not an accurate comparison. Ali fought fair. But it wasn't Pendleton's insults that bothered me; it was knowing I no longer had Molly to turn to. She was always there for me. If only I'd been there for her.

Fingers tapped the driver's side window, jerking me back to the present. A clean-cut young trooper leaned close to the window. "You okay in there, buddy?"

I signaled that I was and glanced at my watch. It was 12:45. Despite the three aspirin I'd swallowed, my head still hurt. I sighed and pondered my next move. I owed Elizabeth a briefing but didn't feel well enough to face her just yet.

Unsure of my next move, I revved the car and headed west on Tudor, thinking I would head home, grab some lunch, and go from there. I glanced up. Blue sky had given way to a somber mass of gray clouds. The weather report I'd heard on the drive from Lake Hood had said to expect snow by nightfall. Snowfall this early in September was not unheard of, but it was rare all the same.

I was about to hang a right onto the Seward Highway when an idea popped into my head. I hooked a left and entered the southbound lane of the Seward Highway. Five minutes later I was on the south end of town near where Potter Marsh begins. I pulled off the highway to the right and slid into a parking space at the Rabbit Creek Shooting Park, where I was greeted with the familiar crack of gunfire. Reaching under the driver seat for my trusty Ruger .357 magnum, I exited the car, popped the trunk lid, and stuffed the pistol into a small black duffel bag. Ten minutes later I had paid the range fee and grabbed a wooden target frame and some paper targets leaning up against the range building.

In my years as a P.I., I'd made it my custom to head for the shooting range whenever I needed to think through a tough case or just recharge my batteries. Perhaps the sound of gunfire blasts out the cobwebs in my brain.

With a cease-fire in progress, I walked up to an empty bench. While the other shooters checked their targets, I set my bag on a small table, removed the Ruger and a pair of ear protectors, and carried a target frame and a fresh target out to the fifteen-yard line.

When the range guide shouted "all clear," I donned my ear protectors, chambered five .38 rounds, and stepped up to the firing line. Though I normally kept the revolver loaded with .357 Magnum shells, I preferred the less powerful—and cheaper—38s for range use. I cocked the gun, took aim at the black bull's-eye at the center of the target, and squeezed the trigger. The resulting *whack!* was muffled into a *whoomf!* thanks to the ear protection.

I reloaded, squeezed off five more shots, and repeated the process twice more. On the command of "cease firing," I walked out to my target, drew circles around the impact holes with a Sharpie to distinguish them from later shots, and returned to the bench to wait for the "all clear."

So much had happened in the ten days since Elizabeth walked through my door, I hadn't really had time to think about it all, but my shooting therapy seemed to be working because I was thinking about it now. My grief at losing Molly had been so all-consuming that I'd lost perspective and focus. This case had forced me out into the world again, shown me that it wasn't all about me. Others had lost as much as I, perhaps more. Elizabeth. Harvey. Maria. Even Joe.

I'd also come to realize how much I'd been missing P.I. work. Case in point: my airplane ride with Joe Meacham that morning. Aside from the pure satisfaction of barfing on his plane, it confirmed—to my satisfaction, at least—that he'd murdered Tom, and that felt pretty damn good.

I hated the man's arrogance, thinking he'd gotten away with it. He seemed to be taunting me, daring me to catch him. The thing was, there was a time when I knew I could, but now, well, I wasn't so sure.

Before Molly died, I'd been confident of my skills, even a bit cocky, but in the months since Molly's death I'd slipped into a funk. I was off my game, screwing up, like the way I'd screwed up the recording. Not that Pendleton would have reopened the investigation anyway. He was more interested in career advancement than justice, which was a pity because the Alaska State Troopers was a damn good organization. Pendleton was right about one thing though. I was unable to answer the question that had been nagging at me since I'd first suspected foul play in Tom Landers' death: How did Joe do it?

The pop and thud of pistol fire trailed off until "All clear!" boomed over the P.A. system. Once again, I walked out to my target, marked up my shots, and returned to the bench to await the next round of fire.

Elizabeth was due for an update. It wasn't going to be pretty. She and Joe had become increasingly chummy since Harvey's death. I wasn't at all sure she was ready to accept that Joe was not the man she thought he was. Still, I had to try. Her safety—maybe even her life—depended on it.

As soon as the command to "Commence firing!" rang out, I picked up the Ruger and took aim. I stuck with it until thirty-five minutes past three. That's when I ran out of ammunition.

My shooting session had been remarkably effective. The nausea and headache were gone, replaced by a ravenous appetite. The only thing I'd had to eat that day was a package of cheese crackers, so I steered the Subaru for a hole-in-the-wall deli I liked on the south side. Roger fixed me up with an Italian sub that lesser artisans only dream of. The place was dead, so he expounded for half an hour on the relative merits of various fly fishing rods. I left there, remarkably refreshed, at 4:30. That left me roughly three hours to brief Elizabeth and get ready for my date with Maria.

The first thing I noticed as I approached Elizabeth's house was a thin layer of termination dust covering everything in sight. The second thing I noticed was Joe Meacham's pickup truck in the driveway. By now he'd have told her about his encounter with me over Cook Inlet. He'd figure I'd have spoken with Elizabeth by now, told her my suspicions about him.

You should have talked to her right away, dumb ass.

I pulled alongside Joe's truck and cast a wary glance at the mountains. I suspected there'd be six inches of new snow at this elevation by morning.

I thumbed the buzzer. When Elizabeth appeared moments later, she didn't seem surprised to see me. I also noticed that she wasn't smiling.

I've got a bad feeling about this.

"Hello, Sidney. Joe and I were about to have dinner." She peered at me intently, her voice cold as the mountain air. "What do you want?"

"We need to talk." I locked eyes with her. "In private."

She glanced over her shoulder. "I have to keep an eye on the kitchen. Can't it wait?"

"I'm afraid it can't. It's about Joe."

Sighing impatiently, she stepped outside, pulling the door shut behind her.

"All right, but please make it quick."

As succinctly as possible, I briefed her on the autopsy report, my interviews of Clint Fargas, Bud Branigan, and Janet Foster, and my encounter with Joe in his plane. Finally, I told her about my efforts to get the state troopers to reopen the case, leaving out my failed attempt at audio recording.

She listened in silence. As I spoke I saw some of the edge come off her coldness, replaced by worry. When I was finished she said, "You really think Joe murdered Tom?"

"I'm afraid it's the only thing that makes sense."

With sidelong glances toward the house she spoke, her voice measured. "Isn't it possible you're jumping to conclusions? It's a pretty big leap to conclude foul play."

"I don't think it is. And my suspicions are supported by what you told me about Tom's wedding ring. Joe as much as admitted it himself when we were flying this morning."

"Did Joe actually tell you he murdered Tom?"

I let out a sigh. "Not in so many words."

She shook her head slowly and flashed a look of defiance. "I'm not buying any of this. I've known Joe for twenty years. I refuse to believe him capable of killing anyone, let alone his best friend."

"Elizabeth, I've seen the rage in him. I assure you he's more than capable."

"I know he has a temper, but that doesn't make him a killer. Since Harvey's passing he's shown me the kind of man he is. Did you know he wants to build a lodge for us on Lake Clark like I've always wanted?"

In the calmest voice I could muster I said, "I've spoken to him twice now and—"

"He says you've been harassing him. Is that true?" Her eyes, so blue and penetrating, seemed to cut right through me.

A soupy mixture of anger and frustration bubbled to the surface. "Elizabeth, he's lying to you!"

She folded her arms. "Let's face it, Sidney, you've had a problem with Joe from day one. You're letting your dislike for the man cloud your judgment."

My heart sank. I needed desperately to regain control of the conversation. "What about Bud Branigan and Janet Foster? They've both seen what he's capable of."

"Bud's always been jealous of Joe's athletic ability," she snapped. He's held a grudge ever since Joe had to let him go. And this Foster woman is a drug addict. I'm surprised you believe anything she says."

Joe had primed Elizabeth in advance of my arrival. He'd known just what to say to turn her against me. Not only had I underestimated her fondness for him, I'd underestimated *him*.

Better get your A Game back, and fast.

"I'm concerned for your safety, Elizabeth. He's not who you think he is."

Her blue eyes turned cold. "We all have our little secrets, don't we?"

I stared at her. "I'm not following."

"I'll try to be more clear. Are you seeing a psychiatrist?"

I took half a step back. "And if I am? What does that have to do with anything?"

"You better than anyone surely understand how the violent loss of a loved one can impair judgment."

I felt what little strength I had left now oozing from my body. "Where is this coming from?"

"I got a call from a Trooper Pendleton this afternoon. He told me some disturbing things about your investigation. That you've been pestering witnesses."

Pendleton. The gift that keeps on giving.

"You hired me to find the truth and I did. Now I'm telling you Joe is a killer. He's dangerous."

She shook her head slowly. "I knew you came with baggage, but I hired you anyway on Eddie Baker's say-so. It seems I made a mistake."

The door creaked open and there stood Meacham, his skyscraper frame filling the opening. He looked at me and a smile appeared, snakelike, along the ridge of his mouth. His husky baritone boomed, "Liz, I think the casserole's done." His gray eyes never left mine.

"I'll be there directly," she said.

"Don't be long," Joe said. He backed into the house, still smiling, and shut the door.

Elizabeth stepped closer. "I've come to like you, Sidney, so please listen carefully to what I have to say. Your wife's tragic suicide has obviously affected you more than you realize. I think it would be best for all concerned if you cease work on my case immediately. You may bill me for your time and expenses. I do appreciate all the hard work you've done. Now, if you'll excuse me, I have dinner to serve."

She retreated into the house and closed the door, leaving me standing there like a damn fool. I walked slowly back to my car, got in, and sat there motionless. How long, I don't know, but after a while, I became aware of a chill running through me and started up the engine. On my way back down the hill, cotton-ball-sized flakes of snow began to fall all around me, melting as they struck the windshield.

Twenty-seven

Elizabeth's words were still ringing in my ears when I pulled into the parking garage at 5:54. I didn't want to go home just yet, so after parking the car I continued past the Mighty Moose, turned right at Fourth Avenue, and sauntered into the Prospector Bar.

The Prospector is a fixture in downtown Anchorage, popular with attorneys and investigators from the Public Defender Agency who congregate there after work to lick their wounds or celebrate their victories, as the case—or cases—may be. More times than I care to remember I had dropped by at the end of the day and ended up getting home far too late.

I slid onto a bar stool and was greeted by my favorite bartender, Daniel "Happy Dan" Dooley, a rail-thin man of about thirty, sporting a bushy black beard and a jovial grin.

"Hey, Sid. It's been a while. What can I get you?"

"Scotch on the rocks."

His raised an eyebrow. "I thought you were a Corona man these days?"

"I'm expanding my repertoire."

"I love to see a man stretch his boundaries."

I plopped a twenty on the bar and peered around the dark interior. There were maybe a dozen customers either sitting at the bar or at one of the half-dozen tables spaced around the floor. A battered old jukebox blared out a country tune. The atmosphere was mellow.

Happy Dan brought my drink and, as he'd often done in the past when he wasn't too busy, stuck around to chat. "So, how's it hangin' on a Saturday night?"

I didn't answer but instead lifted my glass and took a sip.

He watched me intently. "Sid, you don't look well."

"I've had a bad day."

"Wanna talk about it?"

"Well, let's see. I was threatened by a homicidal maniac at three thousand feet, the Alaska State Troopers laughed me out of their building, and my client fired me." I lifted my glass and paused. "Oh, I almost forgot. I have a date tonight that I'm not sure I'm ready for."

"What are you complaining about? At least you have a date."

He watched with bemusement as I sent the remaining contents of my glass to their final resting place and smacked my lips. A nod told him to pour me another. When he returned, I talked and he listened.

"Ever been married, Dan?"

"Nope." He rapped his knuckles on the bar. "That's one mistake I've yet to make."

"Mistake? Marriage is the best thing in the world, my friend."

He nodded, smiling knowingly. I hadn't spoken of Molly much to anyone since her death. Dan was an exception.

I downed a sizable portion of the alcohol in my glass and set it on the bar. I lifted my left hand to his gaze and held it there. "See this ring?"

His face held a meager smile. "Yeah, Sid. I see it."

I rested my elbow on the bar and gripped the silver band between the thumb and forefinger of my left hand as the room began to rotate.

"This ring hasn't left this finger since the day we we were married."

Dan nodded patiently. The man had no doubt listened to more lonely heart stories than there are mountains in Alaska. If there is such a thing as a Bartender's Ten Commandments, commandment number one must be, *Don't interrupt a drunk when he's telling a story.*

"You wanna know something, Dan? She hasn't even been gone a year and I'm already dating. How's that for a schmuck?"

I emptied my glass and he brought me another. I drank half of it as he looked on and the buzz hit me hard. Happy Dan mixes a strong drink.

The thing about getting drunk is that, even as you become increasingly impaired, you retain a certain detached self-awareness. I discerned the slurring of my words, the exaggerated arm movements, the self-pity dripping from my lips.

I tugged at the ring like a bandage I was trying to peel off. "Everyone's telling me it's time to move on." I raised my glass, letting the glow from a pale white lamp behind the bar filter eerily through the liquid. "She was my light and my hope, Dan."

The accumulated mass of all that had happened that day—and in the last year—swept over me. I fought to hold it together, squeezing the glass until I feared it might shatter in my grip. From some far-off place I heard, "Sid."

I lowered the glass to find Dan looking at me.

"How about asking yourself what Molly would want?"

My head was spinning like a horse on a merry-go-round. I croaked out some words that were unintelligible.

He leaned in so close I could hear his breathing. "If the lady loved you half as much as I think she did, she'd want you to be happy."

I think my head hit the bar just then. I'm not sure.

Happy Dan slapped me on the shoulder. "Go home and clean yourself up, buddy. You don't want to be late for your date, man." He grabbed the twenty and my empty glass and walked away.

I grunted a farewell, slid off the barstool, and staggered the two blocks to my apartment. Once inside, I went straight to the bedroom, where I flicked on the nightstand light, removed my shoes, and collapsed on the bed. The alarm clock said 6:35 p.m. I had roughly an hour to shower and head out the door to pick up Maria. I hoped I'd be sober enough to drive by then.

I was about to strip off my clothes and jump in the shower when my gaze fell on the diary lying beside the alarm clock. I rested my palm on the soft leather, drawing it across the surface.

Open it. You know you want to.

I picked it up and pulled back the cover, noting a sweet smell reminiscent of lilacs. The pages were filled with Molly's precise, elegant script. I selected a page at random and read the first entry:

Feb. 17th – Up by 7 a.m. The thermometer reads minus 4. Sid got in sometime early this morning. I expect he'll be on surveillance again tonight. I worry when he's out so late. I wonder if he thinks of me through the long hours. Volunteering this morning. Lunch with P.C.

I slammed the book shut and traipsed into the kitchen. I pulled a Corona out of the fridge, twisted off the cap, arced the bottle to my lips, and stopped.

What the hell are you doing?

I set the bottle on the counter and returned to the bedroom. For the next two minutes, I stared at the diary like it was a chunk of hot plutonium, then picked it up and and read another passage:

March 14th – Sid was home for dinner, what a sweet surprise! The smile when he saw me warmed my heart; his abrupt departure was like a dagger through it. The sunlight slowly returns, and breakup (how appropriate the word for spring in Alaska) I pray is not far off. I do love it here but sometimes I feel so alone.

I bookmarked the page with a finger and, with all the strength I could muster, took my mind back to that day. I forced myself to remember walking through the house calling her name, dragging myself from room to room as that unwieldy feeling of dread gripped me. Finding her lying there, the ribbons of blood spun in all directions, gun on the floor.

I was about to read more when I heard a quiet thump coming from the living room. It sounded like Priscilla jumping off the rocker. *The queen is hungry.* I closed the diary and was about to set it down when I heard another thump, this one different from the first. *What's she gotten into now?*

I placed the diary on the nightstand and started for the living room. The moment I passed through the bedroom door a black blur slammed into me. In one sweeping movement two inhumanly powerful arms encircled my chest, pinning my arms to my sides. I lashed out wildly with both feet but they flailed the air as a deep, menacing voice boomed, "I warned you to keep out of my business!" Ape-like arms compressed my chest inward, forcing life-giving air from my lungs like a human bellows. Pain, like that of a thousand needles, wracked my torso. I gasped for air but none came. I was slipping away, pinpoints of light popping like flashbulbs, darkness falling, falling ...

Light returned. My body twisted and hit the floor hard, the sweet taste of air filling my lungs but with it came a burning like fire and I knew my ribs were broken. I lay there bellowing and heaving. For how long? Seconds? Minutes? I listened in between the rhythmic sounds of my own gasping. The room was strangely quiet. Deathly quiet. *Was he gone?*

I struggled to rise to my feet but the pain in my chest sent tremors rippling through my body and I lay still again, flat on my back. I licked at something warm on my lip—my own blood.

And, then like a specter, he came from somewhere beyond my vision and loomed over me, a huge black paper-doll silhouette. His voice was cold and lifeless. "It was nice knowing you, Reed."

It was otherworldly, like watching a Hitchcock film in slow motion. He crouched down and, with a sweep of his massive arms, seized Molly's rocking chair and raised it above his head. I curled into a fetal position just as my world turned pitch black.

Twenty-eight

We sat in a quaint little bistro, shoppers striding past us, the late afternoon sun streaming down. Molly watched me from across a narrow iron table. She had just said something, but I was too busy watching the sun highlight the freckles that dotted her cheeks.

"Sidney, are you listening to me?"

"Of course."

"Will you be home for dinner?"

I stirred my coffee. "You probably shouldn't wait up."

Her smile retreated into her angelic face. Lines gathered on her forehead. She reached for her cup, raised it to her lips, set it down again. "I don't like you doing surveillance work. It's too dangerous."

"I'll be careful."

"Will you be armed?"

"I keep my gun in my car."

"Have you ever had to shoot anyone?"

The question caught me mid-sip. I put down my cup and looked at her. "No."

"Are you sure?"

"I think I would remember."

"Promise me you won't."

"That's asking a lot. You know how much I'd like to."

"I'm serious. Tell me you won't."

"Okay, I won't. If I can help it."

"You have to promise."

"Your coffee's getting cold."

She withdrew into herself, the cup cradled in her hands. When she came back out she looked at me. "Come back tonight."

"Don't I always?"

"Just promise me."

"I promise."

The lines suddenly deepened and she reached for me. "Sidney?" She began to move away, drifting.

"Molly?" I reached for her.

"Sidney!" Her voice was more strident now, her body retreating, both hands reaching . . .

"Sidney?"

In an instant, Molly, the bistro, all of it evaporated, replaced by intense white light.

"Sidney, it's all right. You're safe."

All at once there was pain and light and a voice. And a face I knew to go with it.

"Maria? What . . ."

I choked out the words, awareness slowly returning.

Maria stood over me. "You've been injured badly."

I could see her clearly now. She said, "Try to lie still."

She stood by the side of the bed wearing an evening dress with blues and reds. Her hair was almost black in the harsh lighting.

"Hospital . . ." I mumbled. My mouth felt as though it were stuffed with cotton. I swallowed. The taste of scotch ringed my tongue.

The Prospector Bar . . . Happy Dan.

I tried to sit up. A sharp pain jabbed my chest and I felt something tugging at my left arm. I traced the plastic tube from the crook of my elbow to the hanging bag, which led me to the wires, the steady beep . . . beep . . . beep. My heartbeat.

Maria was speaking. "You're at Alaska Regional Hospital. Your friend called 911."

My head throbbed. I reached upward but another sharp pain in my chest put an end to further probing in that direction.

"Your head is bandaged. Try to sit still."

"Friend? What friend?"

Rachel Saint George appeared from somewhere in the room and stood on the opposite side of the bed. "Hey, Sid. You gave me quite a scare."

Nausea reared up. I glanced at the drip bag.

"They've got you on morphine," Rachel said. "You should be feeling no pain."

I looked at her. "How did you—?"

My landlady wore her usual attire of jeans, plaid shirt, and smirky grin. "I was tidying up at the Moose when I heard a racket upstairs, like a couple of Sumo wrestlers were going at it. Figured I'd head up there and tell you to keep the noise level at a dull roar. I stepped outside and saw a big guy run down the stairs and duck around the corner. I ran up and found your door wide open and your apartment trashed—" She grinned. "—even more than usual. You were out cold, beneath what was left of an old rocking chair. As soon as I saw the blood pouring out of your head I called 911."

I needed to know one thing. "Priscilla?"

"Cowering under your bed, scared out of her mind. Don't worry, she's fine. I'm getting pretty damn tired of taking care of you."

"Thanks, Rachel." I turned to Maria. "I take it you two have gotten acquainted?"

"You could say that. Rachel's been regaling me with Sidney stories for the past two hours."

My attempt to force a smile failed miserably. "How did you know I was here?"

"When it got to be 8:30 and you hadn't shown up, I began to worry. I didn't have your number so I called the café. It forwarded to Rachel's cell. She told me what happened and here I am."

Rachel spoke up. "After the paramedics came and carted your ass to the hospital, I checked on the cat and then came here."

I asked Maria, "How long have I been here?"

She glanced at her watch. "Almost five hours."

"You've been here the whole time?"

"Of course not. I've been to the lady's room a few times."

Rachel cleared her throat. "*I'll* be in the lady's room if you need me." She turned and scooted out the door.

Maria moved closer. "Joe Meacham did this to you, didn't he?"

Reaching for the memory, I saw Molly sitting at the bistro table and, before that, the face of Happy Dan. I followed the breadcrumbs. "Well, I stopped for a drink at the Prospector Bar ... Walked home ... Started reading Molly's diary ... Wait a minute. What was that about a rocking chair?"

"Rachel said she found you under a busted rocking chair."

Then it all came roaring back in living color: The death grip, hitting the floor, Molly's rocking chair hovering above me.

She said, "Don't worry about that now. Just rest."

I pushed the image away and stared at her, thinking she looked more beautiful than I remembered. "I'm glad you're here."

She placed her hand on the bed near mine. "So am I."

I touched it lightly. She made no effort to pull away.

Rachel's voice broke the silence. "I raided the vending machine. Thought we could use some junk food." She looked at Maria, then me, and grinned. "Bad timing?"

Maria took a step back and swept her bangs to one side. "Sidney and I were just talking. What have you got there?"

Rachel shot me a sly grin and laid a half dozen candy bars on the tray near the bed, keeping one for herself. "Help yourself, guys," she said, biting into a Twix bar. "Just don't tell the nurse where they came from. She seems like a real ball buster."

Just then a middle-aged man with salt-and-pepper hair wearing hospital scrubs appeared. He nodded briefly to my visitors and strode to the side of the bed, clutching a clipboard in his bony white fingers. Maria joined Rachel on her side of the bed.

"Sidney," he said, glancing up from the chart. "I'm Dr. Halperin. You're awake, finally. That's good. How are you feeling?"

"I think you're about to tell me."

"Well, you were pretty banged up when they brought you in. Three fractured ribs and a nasty bump on the head are the worst of it. Some minor cuts and bruises. Somebody messed you up pretty bad. I'm waiting for a few test results, but from what I can see, there's nothing wrong with you that won't heal with the proper amount of rest." He smiled. "You're in pretty good shape for a forty-five-year-old man."

"You don't look so bad yourself, Doc."

The doctor turned to Maria, then Rachel. "Well, his sense of humor appears to be undamaged."

Rachel said, "Is that what you call it?"

Halperin turned back to me. "Get some rest. I'll check back with you in the morning."

"When can I go home?"

He frowned. "You sustained a nasty bump on the head, Sidney. We need to rule out a concussion. I should have those results sometime tomorrow. If everything looks okay, I'll consider releasing you. Even so, you'll need to take it easy for a while. Okay?"

"Thank God I love hospital food."

The doctor turned to leave, then stopped. "Oh, there's a police officer waiting to speak with you. I'll send him in."

"I should probably be going," Maria said. She stepped forward and squeezed my hand. "You owe me dinner, mister."

"I'll try not to get assaulted next time."

She smiled and walked away with a grace of movement I hadn't noticed before.

"I'm out of here, too," Rachel said. "I've got a business to run. Get well soon so we can talk about that train wreck you call an apartment."

No sooner had she gone than a big man came in wearing the dark blue uniform of the Anchorage Police Department. He was clean cut and devoid of a smile.

"Mr. Reed," he said in that authoritative manner they teach new recruits at the academy. "My name is Officer Trueblood. They tell me you were assaulted."

"They tell me that, too." I know how the system works. All 911 calls are routed into the Emergency Operations Center. Depending on the nature of the call, the EOC notifies the relevant parties, in my particular case, the APD.

The officer withdrew a black spiral notebook from a vest pocket and leafed through the pages. From experience, I knew he also had an audio recorder concealed in his vest pocket capturing every word we uttered. I hoped it worked better than the one I used on Joe Meacham.

He found the page he was looking for. "Three broken ribs, numerous contusions and abrasions." He looked at me. "Pretty vicious assault. You mind telling me what happened?"

"Not much to tell. I'd been gone all day. When I got home someone jumped me from behind. Next thing I remember I'm in this bed. That's about it."

He scribbled in his notebook. "Did you get a look at who did this?"

"No, not really."

"Got a name?"

"No."

"Anything else?"

"No."

"That's it?"

"Pretty much, yeah."

He looked at me hard. "What's your occupation, Mr. Reed?"

"I'm retired."

"And before that?"

"I was a private investigator."

"Working on anything now?"

"As I said, I'm retired. I'd like to rest now. Are we done?"

"What do you suppose he was after?"

"No idea."

"Do you own anything of value?"

"I have an antique rocking chair. And a cat."

"Made any enemies?"

"Counting the cable company?"

His ears twitched. "This is a serious matter, Mr. Reed. A man broke into your apartment and almost killed you and you have no idea who or why?"

"That about sums it up."

"Then I guess we're done." He snapped his notebook shut and stuffed it back in his vest. He opened his mouth to speak, then paused. Finally, he said, "I wish you a speedy recovery, Mr. Reed."

I watched him leave the room. Technically, I didn't lie to him. I really didn't see much of anything. But it was Meacham, all right. I'll never forget that voice or those King Kong arms squeezing the life out of me. Not in a million years. But if Joe knew I'd accused him of assault, he might make things difficult for Elizabeth after he bailed out, at a time when she was still grieving over Harvey. And I wanted him arrested for murder, not assault.

I buried my head in fluffy white hospital pillows and stared at the ceiling. My mind drifted to Maria. The touch of her fingers lingered in my thoughts.

Forgive me, Molly.

I closed my eyes and let sleep take me.

Twenty-nine

At ten o'clock Sunday morning I was still yawning myself awake when a short, squat nurse with short-cropped black hair and a bubbly disposition removed the IV from my arm and changed the dressing on my head wound. She promised to return later with pain medicine. Dr. Halperin came in as she was leaving and stood by the bed.

"Good morning, Sidney. How did you sleep?"

"Lying down, same as always."

"I'll have to write that one down," he said with a grin. "I've taken you off the morphine drip. The nurse will give you something for pain."

"When can I get out of here, doc?"

"Well, the good news is, you don't have a concussion."

"And the bad news?"

"There is no bad news, but I would like to keep you one more day to make sure there are no complications with that head wound." Noting my disappointment, he patted my arm. "I'll check in with you first thing in the morning. If everything looks good, you'll be discharged and on your way." And then he was gone.

I switched on the TV and had surfed through all the channels twice when Rachel Saint George walked in. We talked for about twenty minutes, mostly about Priscilla and coffee shop gossip. Then she said, "By the way, I got a call from your client."

"Elizabeth Landers?"

"That's the one. She seemed pretty anxious to reach you. I told her what happened. I hope that was all right."

I told her it was. As she got up to leave she encouraged me to walk around. I promised I would. After she'd gone, I wondered if Maria would stop by. I drifted off to sleep and dreamt that I was kissing her outside the Sullivan Arena while we waited in line to buy tickets for a Beatles reunion concert—John and George had apparently been reincarnated for the performance. The scent of shampooed hair spilled over me and we embraced, oblivious to the crowd squishing us from all sides.

"Sidney?"

My eyelids flapped in the glare of cold white light. When my vision cleared I was staring into the eyes of Elizabeth Landers. Worry clouded her face.

"Elizabeth? What are you—"

"Sidney, I don't know what to say." She fought back tears, her usual stoicism gone for the moment. "Never in my wildest dreams did I think something like this would happen."

I coughed and it hurt like hell. I reached for a paper cup filled with lukewarm water and drank it down. "That's why I get the big bucks."

"Joe did this to you, didn't he?" I set the cup down and looked at her, not saying anything. She dragged a straight-backed chair to the side of the bed, the grating of metal on the tile floor reminding me of fingernails scraping across a chalkboard. I waited while she got settled.

"Yesterday after dinner, Joe left the house in a surly mood. It didn't occur to me that it had anything to do with you. When he returned a few hours later there was a cut on his hand. He said he'd hurt himself working on his airplane, but I knew he was lying. When I pressed him about it, he blew up at me. Said you'd been filling my head with a lot of nonsense about Tom's death." She turned toward the window and the fading light. It suddenly dawned on me that it was late in the day. I glanced at the clock on the opposite wall. It read 5:48.

"Sidney." She was still looking out the window. "I've never seen him so upset."

I started to speak but thought better of it.

"He said I was not to see you again. I told him I would see whomever I damn well pleased, thank you very much." She turned from the window. "I told him to get out and then I tried to call you. I finally got a hold of your landlady. She told me what happened." She paused, sadness washing over her. "You were right about him. After everything that's happened, I wanted to believe he was what I needed." She looked down at her feet, then at me. "About those things I said. I—"

"Already forgotten."

She touched my left hand with hers and I patted it reassuringly.

"You had no way of knowing he'd come after me."

She shook her head. "I should have. If only you could have seen the look in his eyes when he stormed out of the house."

"I've seen it."

"I can't imagine how awful it must have been. He could have killed you."

I nodded slowly. "When he lifted Molly's rocker over his head, I thought—"

I froze in mid-sentence. Something in my brain engaged, like a car that's been dead for months suddenly turning over. It all came rushing back—Joe standing over me, the wild look in his eyes, the animal-like grunt, Molly's rocker arcing toward me . . .

From somewhere far off, Elizabeth said, "Sidney, what is it?"

"When I saw Pendleton yesterday, he said he has a moose head with the victim's blood on it."

"I don't follow."

In my old broken-down-car of a brain, a plan was taking shape. "Pendleton doesn't have the moose head. Joe has it."

"The moose head in his den?"

"Yeah, that one." I glanced up at her. "We have to get it."

Her mouth fell open. "Come again?"

"We have to get that moose head, or at least get a good look at it."

Her face clouded. "Why on earth would we want to do that?"

"Locard's Principle."

She sighed in frustration. "You're not making any sense. Who is Locard?"

I scooted painfully into a sitting position. "The question you should be asking is, who *was* Locard. I'll tell you. Dr. Edmund Locard was the Sherlock Holmes of France. He practically invented the field of forensic science, which can be summed up in Locard's Principle."

"Which is?"

"A criminal always brings something into the crime scene with him and takes something from it when he leaves."

The lines in her forehead deepened. "That's very interesting, Sidney, but I still don't see what this has to do with the moose head in Joe's house."

I felt almost giddy. I didn't think that was possible with three cracked ribs and a busted head. "Elizabeth, listen to me. I know how Joe killed Tom, I know how he staged the crime scene to look like a hunting accident, and I know why Harvey killed himself. And the best part is, I think maybe, just maybe, I can prove it. Will you help me?"

She sat upright in her chair. "What do you want me to do?"

"I need you to get me inside his house."

She stared at me like I'd just descended from another planet. "You're asking me to help you break in?"

"That's exactly what I'm asking."

Her eyes flittered wildly back and forth trying to process it all, then they fell on me, as straight and blue as I'd ever seen them. "All right, Sidney. I don't understand any of this, but I said I would see this through and I meant it. What can I do?"

"Well, we need to come up with some kind of ruse so that I can get inside and have a look around. Maybe we could—"

"I have a key."

"Really?" I said.

"Yes, he gave me one right after Harvey died so I can look in on things for him when he's away on his hunts, but—"

"Great. He'll be leaving for his hunt tomorrow. After I'm released, I'll pick you up at your place and we'll head on over there and—" Her face had darkened as I was speaking. I stared at her. "What?"

"That won't work. He's asked a friend of his to look after the place until he gets back. He'll be getting there sometime in the morning."

I frowned. "Is that normal?"

"No, it's not. He usually drops his dogs off at a kennel and has me or Harvey check on the house every few days. I think you're making him nervous. I'm sorry, Sidney."

The room fell silent as I pondered this new dilemma. My eyes darted to the clock on the wall. It had been a little over three hours since my last pain pill. Soon it would wear off. I looked at Elizabeth, who was looking at her purse, nervously pulling on the strap. I caught her attention and said, "Give me the key."

With a puzzled look she opened her handbag, fumbled around inside, and pulled out a key chain with a bronze-colored fob stamped with the Alaska state flag: gold stars on a blue background representing the Big Dipper and Polaris. A single silver key dangled from the chain. She held it out to me and I wrapped my fingers around the cold metal.

She said, "This only works on the front door. He keeps the back door bolted shut."

Her hand trembled when I took it in mine. "Call Joe. Make a date with him for eight o'clock tonight. Tell him you need to see him. Make something up. I don't care where you go or what you do, just make sure he's out of the house for at least an hour. Can you do that?"

She nodded numbly. "You're crazy, Sidney Reed, but I trust you." She picked up her red handbag, walked to the door, and paused, her features pale and drawn. "Make no mistake about it. If Joe catches you in his house, he *will* kill you. You know that, right?"

I nodded. I knew it only too well.

She turned to go, then stopped and half-turned. "Oh, I almost forgot. He usually ties those beastly dogs of his outside when he leaves the house, but if he doesn't, you won't get past them. If that's the case, just . . . leave, okay?"

I read the worry in her eyes. "I'll cross that chasm when I come to it."

"Promise me you'll be careful?"

"I promise."

She started to walk out, pausing in mid-step. An odd look came over her. "How are you getting out of here? You haven't been discharged."

"I'll think of something."

She walked out, heels echoing down the hall. That was a nice speech I'd given her about Locard. What I hadn't told her was that the odds of Joe's moose head containing evidence of a crime after being stuffed by a taxidermist were probably very slim, and even if it did, the troopers were not likely to listen to anything I had to say. A more likely scenario was me being charged with breaking and entering. Then there was the very real possibility Joe would try to finish what he started on Saturday night.

The shift nurse entered the room and picked up my chart. "And how are we feeling this afternoon, Mr. Reed?"

"Like a million bucks. Will you be bringing me my pain meds soon?"

She checked her watch. "You're due in about thirty minutes. Be patient, Mr. Reed."

"Yes, ma'am. Mind if I take a walk down the hall?"

"That's an excellent idea. Just take it slow. Give your body time to heal." With the nurse looking on, I swung my legs over the side of the bed and eased my aching body into a standing position. I felt dizzy at first.

"Easy does it, Mr. Reed. Would you like to lie back down?"

"I'm fine, but I feel self-conscious with you watching me."

"Are you sure you're all right?"

"I'm sure."

Sitting on the edge of the bed, I kept my eyes glued to her until she left the room. As her footsteps receded down the hall, I stripped out of my hospital garb in self-induced slow motion. The simple act of putting on my shirt and pants produced a series of grunts and groans. When the meds wore off I was going to be one hurting puppy.

I finished dressing, limped from the room, and made for the elevator. Hearing footsteps, I ducked into a patient room moments before the nurse walked by. I slipped out the door and, thirty seconds later, rode the elevator to the lobby. As nonchalantly as I could manage, I crossed the lobby and walked out the main entrance into the looming darkness where, as luck would have it, a cab sat idling. I eased myself inside and rattled off my address to the cabbie, a young Middle-Eastern man with a crew cut and ready smile, which soon faded.

"Man, are you all right? You look all beat up."

"Do you mind hurrying it up? I have to get home and feed the cat."

He chuckled. "Sure, pal."

The ten-minute drive to my apartment felt like an hour, with each bounce of the cab producing a corresponding stab of pain in my chest. When we arrived at the Mighty Moose, I paid the fare and trudged up the stairs to my apartment, each step more agonizing than the last. I opened the door, braced myself, and switched on the light.

I thought the place looked bad *before* the fight. Now it was a wreck: coffee table smashed, chairs and lamps upended, papers scattered around the room. Thankfully, the bookcase with Molly's photograph sitting on top had been spared. My gaze traveled to the corner of the room where Molly's rocker once stood. Priscilla's favorite resting place was now reduced to a pile of kindling several feet from its original location. I inched closer. Dark splotches, like inkblots, dotted the carpet—my blood.

I called out for Priscilla. She came straight away and I picked her up. She folded into my arms, purring loudly. "Sorry about your chair. We'll get it fixed."

I shuffled into the kitchen and washed down four aspirin before turning on the faucet and splashing water on my face. Then I glanced at my watch: 7:26. Cleanup duties would have to wait for another time. I had work to do.

I told Priscilla I would catch her later and headed down the rickety steps to the street below. A cold, crisp breeze surged in off the inlet. The moon had risen plump and brilliant, suspended like an enormous floodlight over the Chugach Mountains. I loped to the parking garage, climbed into the Subaru, and started her up. Shards of pain stung my chest when I reached under the seat for the Ruger. I sat listening to the soft metallic purr of the engine, filled with a quiet determination, like nothing I'd ever known.

Thirty

Joe Meacham's house was bathed in darkness, except for pale yellow slits of light spilling from two small windows. Locating the narrow clearing that had served as my stake-out post two nights earlier, I eased into place and leaned back in my seat to wait for Elizabeth to pick up Joe. The plan—in theory—was simple: Get inside, make my way to the den, examine the moose head, record any evidence I find with my digital camera, and get out of there without being arrested—or shot.

I wasn't too worried about the first part. It was the not-getting-shot part of the plan that bothered me. That, and being ripped apart by his dogs. I hadn't forgotten about the two English Mastiffs. Elizabeth had told me that when Joe was away he always left them tied up outside. I was counting on that to be the case tonight.

At 8:05 twin headlights appeared up the street. Moments later Elizabeth swung her Mercedes into the driveway and honked the horn to signal her arrival, although the dogs were a much more effective signal. The hulking figure of Joe Meacham emerged with his hellhounds in tow. I watched as he muscled his pets into the clearing I'd seen on my two earlier visits, holding each by a long chain attached to its respective collar. He clipped each dog's chain to a metal pipe driven into the ground, a ringbolt attached to one end. So far, so good. At least I wouldn't have to deal with those two monsters inside the house. Outside would be another matter.

His dogs secured, Meacham strode to the passenger side of the Mercedes and got in. As soon as Elizabeth backed out of the driveway and onto the street, I eased my pain-addled body out of the Subaru, took a couple of deep breaths, and checked my jacket pockets for the two pieces of equipment I would need—a flashlight and a point-and-shoot camera—and one that I hoped I wouldn't need—my trusty Ruger. Satisfied, I began my slow walk toward the house.

With only moonlight to guide me, I shuffled silently down the middle of the street in my rubber-soled sneakers. The closest neighbor was several hundred yards away, but I didn't want to test Murphy's Law more than was absolutely necessary, and I certainly didn't want to set those dogs to barking. They would do that soon enough.

As I neared the house, an eerie silence engulfed everything around me. The dogs had fallen silent. With only the aspirin I'd taken to relieve the pain, the aching in my chest and muscles had intensified. I was all too aware that my injuries had left my ability to move and react severely compromised. Should there be any sort of confrontation, I was liable to get my ass kicked again—or worse.

Arriving at the end of Meacham's driveway, I stopped. With shrubbery providing cover, the dogs were still unaware of my presence. I stared silently at the front door—my destination.

What the hell. You only live once.

I said a silent prayer that those dog chains would hold and began walking toward Meacham's front door. I cleared the bushes and five steps later my feet hit the gravel driveway.

Sheer bedlam erupted. First growls, deep and menacing, sliced the night air, sending shivers up and down my spine, followed immediately by frenzied, high-pitched howling. As my feet scuffed gravel, I glanced to my left and saw, in the eerie moonlight, two ghostly shapes barreling toward me, eyes glazed and fiendish, jaws snapping. In the split second it takes to calculate danger, a single horrifying thought gripped me; I didn't know how long their chains were. I burst into a flat-out run, all thoughts of cracked ribs and bruised muscles having evaporated in a burst of adrenaline, propelled by the certainty that if those dogs caught me they would rip me to pieces.

The front door loomed ahead. Sixty feet . . . fifty . . . Their growls intensified . . . Forty . . . thirty . . . I could almost feel their hot breath on my neck. I was ten feet from the door when I heard a loud *oomph!* and the slink of grinding metal as the beasts reached the end of their chains. I turned to see them struggling frantically to regain their footing, feet churning up gravel, frenzied barking echoing in the night. In the time it took to fish the house key out of my pants pocket, they were back on their feet and snapping at me with renewed enthusiasm. They pulled at their chains as if their lives depended on getting their fangs around my throat.

It was like *The Hound of the Baskervilles*, in which Sherlock Holmes and Dr. Watson are pursued by a giant hound. The only thing missing tonight was the phosphorescent glow around their muzzles. Straining to see the keyway in the dim light, I stabbed at the lock until, mercifully, the key slid in and to the right and I stumbled through the door.

The world inside was pitch black. I fished the flashlight out of my jacket and thumbed it on, its circular beam casting an eerie glow around the mudroom. It was just as I remembered it from my visit a few days before. Working the light from side to side, I made my way to the hall and found the door leading to the den with no trouble. I passed through the open doorway and stopped.

My light pierced the room's depth, spotlighting the mounted heads of bear, caribou, and musk ox and casting weird shadows to and fro. Once I had my bearings, I turned the beam toward the space above the fireplace and—

—the moose head was gone. Nothing there now but a bare wall. I moved in for a closer look. I knew I had the right spot— the wall mountings were still in place, and a thin outline of dust recalled its presence. I worked the light around the room in a

360-degree arc. No moose. The beam fell on a door I hadn't noticed before. I opened it and shined my light in to find a small closet crammed with hunting gear—boxes of ammunition, gun cleaning supplies, sleeping bags, but no moose. It was definitely not in the den.

Joe was so proud of that trophy. It was proof of his hunting prowess. He would never get rid of it, unless . . . unless he thought it might implicate him in Tom's murder. Still, it had to be somewhere in the house.

I checked my watch: 8:26—I still had time to look around before getting out of there. Where would he have hid it? Logic told me to look for a basement or crawl space.

I started toward the hallway when my light picked up a glint of metal. It was Joe's .375 H&H Magnum, the big bore rifle he said he'd used to dispatch the moose that killed Tom. I couldn't help but grin. Joe Meacham, great white hunter. I took a step and stopped. A fresh thought entered my pounding head.

Locard's Principle.

I walked over to where the rifle leaned against the wall where I'd first seen it days before. If Locard was right and if my theory about Tom's death was correct, there would still be minute traces of blood on the rifle, regardless of how thoroughly Joe had cleaned it. Picking it up by the barrel, I looked up and down the length of it. I flipped it around so the butt end was facing up, held the light close, and squinted at the finely crafted stock. I peered intently at the butt plate—a black, oval-shaped chunk of steel about four inches long, screwed into the end of the stock—looking for any sign of blood residue hiding in the grooves. I stared blankly at the butt plate. Like a slap in the face, it dawned on me what I was looking at.

I'll be damned.

One of the things I've always loved about this job is that the thing you're looking for often turns out to be entirely different from the thing you thought you were after.

I pulled the digital camera out of my jacket and, using my flashlight for illumination, clicked off half a dozen photos of the rifle, stock, and butt plate, taking care to get a clear shot of the rifle's serial number.

I double-checked my work using the camera's digital display, careful to avoid a repeat of my screw-up with the recorder. Satisfied with the results, I stowed the camera and checked my watch. It was 8:38. I smiled. Plenty of time to get out of there before Elizabeth and Joe returned.

I turned toward the door and froze. The faint yet unmistakable sound of rubber on gravel stung my ears—a car was pulling into the driveway.

They're back.

Thirty-one

Standing in the middle of Joe Meacham's den, my mind raced a mile a minute. The hellhounds, who had by this time quieted down, were going ballistic all over again. A car door slammed.

I am so fucked.

There was only one thing to do. Cupping one hand over the end of the flashlight to dim its light, I raced to the closet, stepped inside and closed the door. I stood at attention, the silence broken only by my own labored breathing. The feathery hum of voices drifted into the closet.

Shifting my feet, I stepped on something soft. My left foot gave way and I stumbled against a wall. Reaching out to brace myself, I lost my grip on the flashlight. I stifled a grunt as the heavy aluminum cylinder caromed off my right foot.

The voices grew closer. The flashlight was still on, casting a faint glow somewhere near my feet. I stooped to get it but was too off-kilter, so I twisted my broken body like a corkscrew and somehow managed to regain a modicum of balance in the cramped space. I was about to retrieve the runaway flashlight when a sliver of light appeared beneath the door.

They're inside the den.

Meacham was saying, "I can take care of you, Liz. You know I can."

Elizabeth replied, "It's not that, Joe. I have no doubt you'd be a good provider."

"What is it then?" His tone was pleading. It was a side of him I hadn't seen before.

"Do I really have to explain it to you, Joe? For heaven's sake,

Harvey's been dead scarcely a week. I haven't even gotten over the shock of it yet."

"So, it's a question of timing then? I can wait, Liz. However long it takes."

"Oh, Joe." Her voice was thick with pity.

"Please trust me, Liz." There was a pause and then he said, "I'll get that drink." Heavy footfalls receded from the room.

I eased the door open and stumbled out of the closet, squinting under the bright lights.

Elizabeth stared in disbelief. "Sidney?" She looked elegant in white chiffon. Clasping a hand to her chest, she whispered, "You scared me half to death. If Joe should catch you . . ."

"What happened? You were supposed to keep him out of the house for at least an hour."

"Believe me, I tried, but he insisted on returning." Her eyes darted around the room apprehensively. "We've got to get you out of here."

"I'm open to suggestions."

She glanced about anxiously. "I'll have to—"

Joe's stomping feet reverberated down the hall and my heart sank. I said, "It's too late. He's coming back."

I slipped into the closet and eased the door shut moments before Joe re-entered the room. A rolled-up sleeping bag served as a passably good chair. Joe's voice boomed.

"Here you go, my dear. Your Bloody Mary."

"Thank you."

Shuffling noises followed.

Great. They're getting comfortable. I'll be in here all night.

"You know, Liz, after this next hunt I'll be in a position financially to start building that lodge for us on Lake Clark. We can do it now. Live there together."

"I don't know," she said, worry in her voice. "I need time."

"I've waited twenty years, Liz. I can't live without you anymore."

This guy makes me sick.

"That's very sweet, Joe. I'm sure things will work out. Why don't we call it a night and talk about this tomorrow?"

Good, get rid of him.

"But you just got here. What's gotten into you tonight?"

"It's nothing. I'm just feeling a little tired. It's been a long day."

"It's that P.I., isn't it?" Meacham's voice rose in anger. "He's been snooping around, filling your head with all sorts of nonsense about Tom."

"Is that why you attacked him in his apartment?"

Careful, Elizabeth. You don't want to go there.

"He has no right to meddle in our lives!"

"Damn it, Joe, you could have killed him."

"I wish I had. I'm not going to let some private dick come between us."

"What are you going to do, Joe? Finish what you started?"

After a breathless pause, he said, "If I have to."

Holy hell.

Elizabeth's anger was making her confrontational. This could turn ugly. I thrust my hand into my jacket and gripped the Ruger.

Here we go.

I sucked in a deep breath of air and burst into the den.

Elizabeth and Joe jumped to their feet. Joe looked like he'd seen the ghost of Harvey Kahill. "Reed? What the hell?"

"I didn't have a chance to thank you for redecorating my apartment." I touched my hand to my chest. "And my anatomy."

"You broke into my house, you son of a bitch."

"What's good for the goose."

"I'm calling the police." He turned toward the door.

"Please do. I'm dying to tell them all about your visit to my place last night."

He stopped and glared at me, his expression morphing from anger into curiosity. Glancing at Elizabeth, his brow furrowed. "Funny. You don't seem all that surprised to see him, Liz."

Elizabeth backed up a step, hands clutching her cherry red handbag.

He moved a step closer to her. "I keep my doors locked. You're the only one except me who has a key." A light seemed to switch on in that big cranium of his. "You gave him the key to my house?"

Elizabeth stood her ground.

Joe looked like someone spilled beer on his favorite rifle. "Liz, how could you?"

I stepped forward. "Cut the crap, Joe. You killed Tom and I can prove it. What do you say we head over to the state troopers and let one of the nice officers on duty take your statement?"

He smiled thinly. "You're a funny guy, Reed, I'll give you that. Tell you what, how 'bout you get your ass out of my house right now and I won't call the police?" The smile faded, replaced by a scowl. "Better yet, how about we finish what we started yesterday?"

He started toward me but hit the brakes when I plucked the Ruger out of my jacket. His sullen gray eyes widened and then rolled to his left where, not five feet away, the Remington leaned against the wall, its barrel glistening.

"Did you know," he said coolly, "that in Alaska, if you shoot an intruder, they won't even arrest you?" He did a slow shuffle toward his rifle. "They call it defense of life and property."

"Don't you want to know how I figured it out?"

"There's nothing to figure out!" He turned to Elizabeth. "Your P.I. friend here is out of his mind. He's seeing a psychiatrist, for chrissake."

She looked at me, her face strangely calm. "I'd like to know." She eased into the couch and glanced up at Meacham. "Sit down, Joe."

"This is my house, Liz."

With a quickness that belied his size, Joe snatched up the rifle and spun around.

"Stop right there!" My command sent a thunderbolt of pain racing through my body.

Meacham froze, the rifle clutched in his meaty hands. "You don't have it in you, Reed."

I gritted my teeth. "Let's find out."

Joe's smug look faded.

I fought to hold the gun steady. "I think you should do what the lady says. After you put the rifle down, of course."

The next ten seconds felt like ten minutes. My heart beat like a hummingbird's. With slow deliberate movements, Joe leaned the rifle against the wall and retreated to the couch. I watched his every move as he settled in next to my client.

"That's better." I took a deep breath and said to Elizabeth. "You asked me to find out why Harvey killed himself, but as I looked into his life, it made no sense. He had everything a man could want: successful business, good friends—" I glanced at Joe. "Beautiful woman." His neck muscles twitched. "It all kept coming back to the hunting trip."

"Jesus, Reed," Joe said. "The troopers ruled Tom's death an accident."

"I know. I read the autopsy report. Have you ever read an autopsy report, Joe?"

He scowled but said nothing.

"Curiously, it said Tom wasn't wearing his wedding ring at the time of his death."

He rolled his eyes. "So what?"

Elizabeth glared at him. "Will you stop interrupting!"

Joe's shoulders drooped. I fought back a smile.

She said, "Go on, Sidney."

"I didn't think too much about it until I remembered you saying Tom always took off his wedding band before he went to bed and put it back on first thing in the morning."

Her eyes widened. "That's right. His fingers would swell up at night."

"That told me Tom must have died in the evening, *after* he took off the ring. In other words, the moose attack story Joe fed the troopers was pure, unadulterated bullshit."

The look on her face reminded me of a mother who'd just caught her son stealing licorice from the local five and dime. Joe was the son.

"That doesn't prove anything, Liz. He could have taken it off prior to the hunt."

Elizabeth answered him with an icy stare.

"Luckily for you," I said, "the troopers failed to grasp the significance of the ring and bought your story. You must have been pretty proud of yourself."

Meacham watched me with hate-filled eyes. I tightened my grip on the Ruger as ripples of pain tore at my chest. I wasn't sure how much longer I could remain on my feet. Beads of sweat ringed my face.

"What I couldn't figure out was how you killed him and then staged the crime scene to look like an accident. It wasn't until I was flat on my back in the hospital and remembered you slamming Molly's rocking chair into me that I put it all together. There you were, Three Amigos sitting around the campfire and drinking brewskies, bullshitting about the moose you'd killed that day. Or was it Tom who shot it? In any event, something made you snap. Maybe you got sick of hearing Tom brag about the moose or maybe you didn't like the way he was talking about Elizabeth. Whatever it was, you lost it. You picked up something—I'm betting it was that rifle—and you hit him with it. How many times did you hit him, Joe?"

Elizabeth buried her face in her hands and sobbed quietly.

Joe's head swiveled from Elizabeth to me, eyes ablaze. "Stop it. You're upsetting her!"

I ignored him. "Now you had a problem. How were you going to explain Tom's death to the troopers? Then it came to you. It was brilliant, really. You saw the severed moose head lying there and realized there was a way out of the hole you'd dug for yourself. You picked it up and slammed it down on him again and again—"

"Stop it!" Elizabeth jumped to her feet. "Sidney, please. I beg you."

I felt sorry for her but I had the floor, and I wasn't finished.

"Now all you had to do was get your story straight for the troopers. I don't imagine it took much threatening to get Harvey on board. When my friend Pendleton showed up and found a moose with blood on its antlers and a hunter with severe head and chest trauma, he reached the obvious conclusion. It wouldn't be the first time a moose killed a man. No reason to suspect foul play. The one potential problem you had was if the troopers asked to see the kill site, but Mother Nature solved that problem for you. It snowed overnight. The M.E. ruled Tom's death an accident. You were in the clear . . . or so you thought."

Joe watched me like a rabid dog itching to lash out.

"There was one problem you never anticipated." I turned to Elizabeth. "Unlike Joe here, Harvey had a conscience. He couldn't live with the guilt of seeing Tom murdered and not being able to stop it or even talk about it, not even to you. Two years of living with that and he couldn't take it anymore. Joe must have suspected he was about to crack. He realized he had to do something before Harvey talked to somebody."

Tears flooded her blue eyes. "It all makes sense. His strange behavior. The suicide note. Poor Harvey."

I looked at Joe. "You took Harvey to Skilak Lake three weeks before his suicide. I'm guessing you reminded him to keep his mouth shut. That he was an accessory to murder. You go down, he goes down with you. I wonder, did you threaten to hurt Elizabeth if he talked?"

"You're living in a fantasy world, Reed. You need help. I told you the man's crazy, Liz. It's time I put a stop to this." He took half a step forward but stopped when I waved the gun.

"I'm not done," I said gruffly.

Elizabeth had stopped sobbing and now sat ramrod straight. "Don't stop, Sidney. I want to hear it all."

Joe's eyes were locked on the Ruger. I could taste the sweat rolling off my cheek. "Harvey felt he had no way out so he made a decision. He chose McHugh Creek to do the deed. It must have held a special significance for him."

Elizabeth spoke up. "It was our favorite place to go hiking. He proposed to me by the creek."

Sweet Jesus.

An overwhelming weariness gripped me. "Twice he drove there to end it and twice he lost his nerve. He found it the night I followed him." I swept away the image of Harvey sticking the gun in his mouth. "With Tom gone, Joe figured he had you all for himself. He hadn't counted on you falling for Harvey. Knowing Joe's pathology, I suspect he did his best, in both subtle and unsubtle ways, to push Harvey over the edge, although we'll probably never know."

Joe stood up. "You can't prove a damn thing."

"Oh, I think I can."

He gestured toward the empty space above the fireplace, his face contorted in a twisted grin. "The head's gone, Reed. I burned it this afternoon. Your little expedition tonight was a big waste of time. I win, you loose."

I glanced at the wall. "Oh, that thing? I doubt very much that trophy of yours contained any evidence tying you to Tom's murder. But I'll bet a weekend on Maui your rifle does."

Joe glanced at the Remington, his smile fading. "What are you talking about?"

"The butt plate on the stock of that rifle is engraved with a series of parallel ridges, known as knurls. When you whacked Tom in the face, those ridges left a transfer pattern on his skin. They're described in the autopsy report. I saw those same marks when I examined your rifle. The lab boys should have no problem coming up with a match. I'll bet they also find traces of Tom's blood on the butt plate. Blood is notoriously hard to wash off. But look on the bright side, Joe. At least Alaska doesn't have the death penalty."

"You're bluffing." He tried to sound confident, but the cracks in his voice told a different story.

"Think so? Let's take it to the lab and find out."

Joe's head swiveled from me to Elizabeth, speechless. My client had been oddly silent, but now she rose, her hands clasped tightly to the top of her handbag. "You killed Tom, you son of a bitch. You killed Harvey, too, just as surely as if you'd pulled the trigger yourself. All these years I trusted you. Tom and Harvey trusted you. Sidney tried to tell me, but I refused to believe him. But now I see the truth."

As she spoke, Joe's bluster and bravado vanished like smoke in the wind. His once booming and resonant voice was now pathetic and frail. "Tom was never any good for you, Liz. Neither was Harvey. You know that. They could never—"

The blast was deafening. My body jerked reflexively, shooting pain through my chest. Then my eyes fell on the revolver clutched in Elizabeth's white-knuckled right hand, its barrel aligned with a small dark circle tattooed on Joe's shirt, directly over his heart.

I hadn't seen it coming, focused as I was on Joe. Hadn't seen my client quietly open her red handbag, reach in, and pull out the revolver.

Joe hadn't seen it either. His weathered face with its dull gray eyes gaped in disbelief. His mouth hung open, voice straining to sputter out words but nothing came except flecks of spittle. A stream of wine-dark fluid oozed from the hole in his chest. He staggered back against the fireplace, paused, and slid down the grate, his long legs folding beneath him, hands reaching upward like a giant praying mantis, knees slamming the hardwood floor. His torso hovered there momentarily, as if suspended by invisible strings, and then he collapsed, face first, onto the floor with a resounding thud.

We stood in stunned silence, watching the life ebb from his body like air from a deflating tire. A pool of blood mushroomed from beneath his prone body. When the dark liquid had almost reached the tip of Elizabeth's left shoe, she jerked it away, a move that seemed to shock her into sensibility. She turned to face me, dazed, the gun turning with her. She murmured, "Is he dead?"

Side-stepping the barrel of the gun, I encircled her wrist with one hand and grabbed hold of the gun barrel with the other. Her trembling hand released its grip on the weapon and I placed it on the coffee table. Wordlessly, I crouched beside the supine figure, mindful of the widening pool of blood. I pressed my index finger to the side of his neck.

"Is he dead?" she repeated, voice quivering.

I stood up on wobbly legs. "Yeah, he's dead."

She stared at his body, lips parted. What does one say at a time like this? I didn't have a clue. I tried to think of something comforting.

"He was a bad guy, Elizabeth."

Dumb, Sidney. Really dumb.

She kept staring.

"Okay, listen," I said. "I need to call 911. There will be questions. We should—"

"No, Sidney." Her voice was soft, almost distant, as she stared down at Meacham.

I placed a hand on her shoulder. "You've been through a lot. Let me take—"

"No!" she repeated, as if I hadn't heard her the first time, and I really hadn't. She turned to face me, her blue eyes locked onto mine. "I know you're just trying to do the noble thing, but right now I need you to leave."

I stared at her in disbelief. "Elizbeth, let's talk about—"

"Please, leave right now. I'll call 911. When the police get here,

I'll tell them what happened. How Joe's behavior had become increasingly erratic since Harvey's death. His angry outbursts, the mood swings. How, after I rejected him, he flew into a rage and lunged at me. Thank God I managed to get the gun out of my handbag in time." The hint of a smile touched her lips. "I had no choice."

I stared at her in amazement. While I was still figuring out which way was up, she had worked it all out. She knew the story she had to tell, knew my being there would only complicate things, for her and for me.

You're not going to rescue the damsel in distress this time, Sid.

"Elizabeth, I—"

She leaned forward and kissed me softly on the cheek. "Please, just go. I beg you."

I nodded slowly. "Okay."

Her sad eyes traced a line from my bruised face to the white swath of bandages encircling my chest. "Thank you, Sidney. You're a good man. Don't ever forget that."

There was so much I wanted to tell her but this was not the time, so I squeezed her hand and went to collect my flashlight from the closet. I scanned the room, knowing there would be no coming back to this house. Satisfied I'd left nothing behind, I walked to the door and turned to see Elizabeth staring at Meacham's lifeless body. She looked at me, then she reached into her bright red handbag and pulled out her cell phone.

Thirty-two

Rachel Saint George inspected my broken body, starting with my bandaged head and working her way down to my suede-wrapped feet.

"Poor Sid," she said with genuine sincerity. "How are we feeling today?"

"Much better, thanks."

It was 10 a.m. Tuesday morning. Following my ordeal Sunday night, I'd gone home and settled into bed, only to endure a night of sleepless agony as I wrestled with the pain in my head and chest and the memory of what happened that night. On Monday morning, after swallowing a fistful of aspirin and my pride, I drove to the emergency room at Alaska Regional where, in exchange for treatment, I endured a lecture on the impropriety of leaving the hospital without being properly discharged. It was worth it though. I was back home by noon, wrapped in fresh bandages, splayed out on the couch, surrounded by pill bottles and feeling no pain.

Late Monday afternoon Rachel came upstairs to check on me. Over my objections she cleaned house—mopping up bloodstains, righting overturned furniture, sweeping up broken glass. At my request she stacked the splintered pieces of wood that had been Molly's rocker in a relatively neat pile in the corner where it once stood. Absent her favorite perch, Priscilla reluctantly relocated to the couch.

Up to that point I'd willfully ignored the ringing of the telephone, but by late Monday I felt well enough to check the answering machine. There were half a dozen messages, mostly from well-wishers who'd heard about my hospital stay. As I played through them I recognized the beguilingly soft lilt of a female voice. "Hi Sidney. It's Maria. I went to the hospital last night, but you'd already been discharged. I hope you're feeling better. When I heard your client had killed Joe Meacham, I couldn't believe it. I'm putting together a story for tomorrow's paper. This whole thing just blows me away. I guess now we'll never know if he really killed Tom Landers." After a pause she said, "Listen, I enjoyed watching his house with you the other night. I . . . I'm sorry for running out on you like I did. Okay, well, I have a deadline to meet. Call me." I fought the urge to call her back. Maybe later.

Having gotten six whole hours of uninterrupted sleep, and lured downstairs by the siren call of the cocoa bean, I felt like a new, if somewhat broken, man.

I motioned toward the espresso machine. "Any life left in that old relic?"

"Just a little." Rachel reached for the handle. That model of modern engineering sprang to life, whipping a large mug of fresh brew into a steaming froth. Idly she said, "So, what's next on the agenda, master detective?"

I pretended to ponder the question. "Alaska winters suck. I'm thinking about moving to Arizona. Or Florida."

"Oh, really? Well, let me remind you that under your lease agreement, I require thirty days' notice. Anyway, you won't leave. You love it here too much." She paused. "And then there's the matter of a certain woman . . ."

"I don't know what you mean."

"I'm pretty sure you do." Rachel slid the mug across the counter. "This one is on the house."

"Thanks, Rachel."

I took my first comforting sip as she pushed a folded-up newspaper in my direction.

"Here. While you're dreaming of sunny Arizona you can catch up on the news. Interesting story on page one."

Drink and paper in hand, I moved sloth-like to a seat by the window, sidling past two twenty-something guys wearing suits and ties. I lowered my aching body into a chair, opened the paper, and immediately knew I wasn't going to need caffeine to perk me up this morning. The front-page headline hit me right between the eyes.

Local man shot dead in domestic dispute

By Maria Maldonado

One man is dead following what police are calling a domestic dispute at a south Anchorage home late Sunday night.

Joseph Meacham, 38, owner/operator of an Anchorage-based guide service, was pronounced dead at the scene from a single gunshot wound to the chest. According to an APD spokesman, Elizabeth Landers, 39, of Anchorage, was visiting Mr. Meacham at his home when an altercation ensued. Although details are still sketchy, Mr. Meacham reportedly became violent and attacked Ms. Landers.

"Perceiving a threat to her life," the spokesman said, "Ms. Landers fired a single shot from a handgun she carried for personal protection. The bullet pierced Meacham's heart, killing him instantly."

An autopsy is scheduled for Wednesday.

District Attorney Grant Fellows told the Daily News, "The state has no plans to file charges at this time. We believe Ms. Landers acted in self-defense."

In declining to file charges, Fellows noted that Mr. Meacham had a history of domestic violence and was a suspect in an assault on a local man on Saturday. He would not say whether the two incidents were related.

Mr. Meacham's death is the latest in a string of tragedies to befall Ms. Landers. Two years ago her husband, Tom Landers, was attacked and killed by a moose during a hunting trip. Less than two weeks ago, a close friend, Harvey Kahill, committed suicide at the McHugh Creek Recreation Area south of Anchorage.

There is no funeral planned for Mr. Meacham, who has no surviving family. Burial arrangements have yet to be announced.

"What a woman," I muttered, laying the paper aside. Outside, freshly fallen snow sparkled in the morning sun as commuters scurried about their day, flattening the white stuff into mush. I longed for Molly to pass by and flash me that smile I loved so much.

"Hi, Sidney."

Maria Maldonado stood over me with a newspaper in one hand and a paper cup in the other. Her chocolate-drop eyes were shining. I smiled as she slid into the chair opposite me. "How are you? I was worried when you didn't call me back."

My hand went to my chest. "All the parts are still intact."

"I'm glad." Her voice was warm and soothing.

I looked at her. "I should have called."

She waved it off and glanced at my newspaper. "Have you read it?"

"Just finished. Nice piece. Well written, factual, concise. Your journalism professor would be proud."

"Oh, shut up!" She settled back into her seat and sipped from her cup. "Pretty strange story, don't you think? Bizarre hunting accident, bizarre suicide, and now this." She took another sip and gave me a look tinged with mischief. "Kind of makes you wonder."

I sipped some mocha.

She leaned forward, her brown eyes big enough to get lost in. Her voice fell to barely a whisper. "There's more to this story, isn't there? You know something. I can smell it."

"I didn't shower this morning."

She groaned. "Come on, Sidney. You're not getting off that easy. What really happened in that house?"

I leaned in, elbows on the table. "You're right, Maria. I do know something."

Her eyes grew wider still. "Yes?"

"I know this great Italian place on the south side. I thought maybe you and I could have dinner there Friday night."

She leaned back and sighed, lips curled up in a fake pout. "How do I know you'll show up this time?"

I looked at her, a smug look on my face, and smiled.

Acknowledgments

This book was first conceived when I was living in Alaska a dozen years ago, but its roots can be traced to my freshman-year English class. So, in a very real sense, this novel began with you, Nancy Dunham. Thank you for making me believe I could write stories.

Marty Kruse, long-ago editor of the Port Clinton *Daily News*, taught me more about writing than he will ever know. Wherever you are, thank you.

I would never have made it past the first draft without the support and encouragement of my Alaska writer's group cohorts, Shanae Branham and Richele Huntington. You're the best.

For their valuable comments and insights, I wish to thank Lana Ayers, Meredith Beck, James and Michele Bighouse, Patty Cable, Dick Dunham, Tepp Dunham, Denise Miller, Kurt Landefeld, Bob Norgard, Peggy Norgard, Sarah Norgard, and Patrick O'Keeffe. To the many others who read the manuscript and provided feedback, my sincere thanks.

To Karin Norgard, the best editor a writer could ever have, thank you for your patience, skill, and love.

I also want to thank my friends and colleagues at the Firelands Writing Center for their faith, hope, and encouragement.

And finally, my sincere thanks to Larry Smith at Bottom Dog Press who has been inspiring and nurturing writers for more than three decades. Thank you for helping to bring *Trophy Kill* into the world.

About the Author

R.J. Norgard grew up so close to the Lake Erie shore, his feet are still wet. He has worked as a newspaper reporter, photographer, and private investigator. He also served twenty years as a counterintelligence officer and agent in the U.S. Army, with tours in exotic places like Alaska, Germany, and Las Vegas, which he thought was too hot. When he's not writing, he's likely messing around in boats, reading, playing tennis, or working on some local volunteer project. *Trophy Kill* is his first novel.

A Note to the Reader

If you enjoyed *Trophy Kill*, please tell others and consider posting a reader review online. And be sure to watch for the next installment in the Sidney Reed mysteries, *Road Kill*, scheduled for release in 2020.

You can visit me online at www.rjnorgard.com and on Facebook at www.Facebook.com/rjnorgard.